# A ROSE TO A KILL

# A ROSE TO A KILL

## GARY LAPERGOLA

Copyright © 2013 by Gary LaPergola.

| Library of Congress Control Number: | | 2012918278 |
|---|---|---|
| ISBN: | Hardcover | 978-1-4797-2609-7 |
| | Softcover | 978-1-4797-2608-0 |
| | Ebook | 978-1-4797-2610-3 |

All rights reserved. No part of this book may be reproduced or transmitted in any form or by any means, electronic or mechanical, including photocopying, recording, or by any information storage and retrieval system, without permission in writing from the copyright owner.

This is a work of fiction. Names, characters, places and incidents either are the product of the author's imagination or are used fictitiously, and any resemblance to any actual persons, living or dead, events, or locales is entirely coincidental.

This book was printed in the United States of America.

Rev. date: 3/15/2013

**To order additional copies of this book, contact:**
Xlibris Corporation
1-888-795-4274
www.Xlibris.com
Orders@Xlibris.com
52812

## SPECIAL THANKS: TO

Tim + Cinny

P.C.

Weezy

Jean

# CHAPTER 1

Cerknica, in the province of Slovenia, is a small village nestled along the base of a mountain. With a population of 450, Cerknica throughout history has been considered a very prosperous and stable little town. The people there are the salt of the earth, hardworking with dirt under their fingernails. No one could ever say that the people of Cerknica were lazy and disrespectful of nature. In fact, they were so proud of their little paradise that every stranger who wandered into town was usually engaged in conversation with one of the townsfolk within minutes after their arrival. "We live in the most beautiful village in all of Europe," they would declare. "No crime, no corruption, and we clean our front steps every morning. So clean is our town that one could eat off the streets." And so it goes in Cerknica, the people never move away, for they are content and well looked after. Generation after generation have come and gone with little or no change.

Now Cerknica Mountain is no ordinary mountain. Legend has it that there is a witch who lives there and had for centuries. As far back as four hundred years ago, a young woman called Monica was an inhabitant of the town, but she lived on the outskirts near the base of the mountain, along the River Dobra.

The river is and was as clear as crystal and teaming with all types of wildlife. Every kind of species of freshwater fish known to man and reptiles live in the river. It is written in the town history archives that the one called Monica was widely known as a witch or something of the sort. That she practiced a religion that went way beyond the teachings of Christianity. That she used incantations for everything, from home remedies, maladies of all sorts, jilted lovers to get revenge, or simply a love potion to bring two people together. Monica was the talk of the town. She existed in the minds of the townspeople as larger than life. But mostly, Monica wanted to be left alone. She practiced her religion with the utmost diligence and passion. Sorcery was the common staple of the Cerknicians when they referred to Monica and her beliefs. Call it what you want, the people were simply afraid of Monica, the witch.

In spite of this, people would come from far and wide, from all over Yugoslavia to see Monica, to seek out her powers. She was famous for her magic powers to ward off diseases and common maladies. Lumbago, poison ivy, and pimples on a young boy's face were treated by Monica. She could cure anything, this sorceress. Anything. But truthfully, Monica possessed a great understanding of herbs and plants, nature's natural healers. Plants that grew in everyone's backyard and in the fields that seemed to stretch forever surrounding Cerknica. She would concoct a potion that when ingested could remove the hair off a wild boar. So strong were her concoctions that most people had to be coaxed and persuaded to visit the witch. One day, a young boy called Milan came to Monica to seek out the powers of this witch to help mend his broken heart. It was the case of a jilted lover, girl meets boy. Girl grows tired of boy and finds someone else. "Drink this magic potion." Monica cackled. Her comedic side would often come out under these circumstances. She would change her voice to sound like a witch on purpose just to give them what they wanted to hear. Truth be told that Monica had the voice of an angel. A high-pitched soprano voice, one that could make a grown man cry. It was said that she could be heard singing like a bird, her soft voice drifting above the mountaintop, soaring like an eagle. No one suspected that it could be Monica, the witch singing such a rhapsody. "Go on, drink up, young Milan, and your broken heart will be mended." "Drink, drink, drink!" she screamed and began to sway back and forth until the boy absorbed the rhythm of her gyrating body. Captivating she was, dressed in black when she performed these rituals of sorcery. "Now be gone with you, and leave a few dinars while you are at it. A witch has to eat too, you know. Go and don't ever come here again for bad luck will descend upon you."

It was widely known that Monica was considered the most beautiful woman in all of Slovenia and perhaps even all of Europe. Every woman in Cerknica was insanely jealous of this mysterious beauty. She had hair the color of a raven, black as night. Her hair was so straight and long that often she would tread upon it with her own feet. Her skin was the color of ivory. So pale yet strikingly beautiful. Her lips were full and beguiling. Some said that her mouth could beckon you without uttering a word. Yes, Monica was certainly a beauty. She could melt the heart of any man and mystify any woman at the same time. Monica enjoyed this attention and loved to sit upon her golden pedestal. She loved being called a witch.

Everyone knew everyone's personal affairs in Cerknica. You could often overhear someone's conversation right outside your window. It is such a small town. Late one November, almost four hundred years ago before a harvest moon, the whispers throughout the town were that Monica had simply vanished without a trace. Some of her more ardent followers came to her neat little cottage at the base of the mountain to search for the witch. "She has disappeared," they proclaimed. "Maybe she accidentally drank one of her potions," they joked. But really, some of the townsfolk were desperately concerned. For Monica provided them with entertainment in their boring little town, in their boring little lives. "The witch may be gone forever," they feared.

The followers searched the grounds around the cottage only to find a silver heart-shaped locket. Inside the locket was a picture, or drawing, of a single black rose. The searchers soon gave up looking for her. Those that hated and feared her rejoiced at the news that the witch was probably dead. Cerknica would no longer live in fear of the dreaded sorceress.

Some months had passed, and a young lad named Igor was walking along the River Dobra, drifting along the path that led him to Lake Bled, the beautiful lake at the base of the mountain. He marveled how every year, right before Halloween, this lake would simply disappear into the ground. *How can this be?* he thought. *Where does all the water go? Oh well, that is just the way it is.* The disappearing lake of Cerknica is and was known far and wide.

As Igor was ambling along the path, he happened to glance over toward a wooded area near a clearing at the edge of the tree line. This area was adorned with lovely fir trees that, for Igor, seemed to grow as high as the heavens. These trees are only found in this part of the world, a peculiar fact that no one quite fully understood. Then again, no place on earth had a witch like Monica. Igor was a curious young man and quite the student in school. It wasn't unusual for one of the other children to ask him a school-related question or to even copy his notes or his homework. Yes, Igor was a very observant boy and liked to think of himself as quite the scholar. This he thought would make him popular with the girls in the village. Yes, intelligence is a virtue. Little did Igor know at the time that he was about to make the discovery of his sweet short life. For there in the clearing he saw something that made the hairs stand up on the back of his neck. *It looks like someone has started a fire*, he thought. *Maybe someone had some old soiled clothes they wanted to get rid of,* he wished. But his instincts told him differently. It looked like nothing he had ever seen before. And even though he was only nine years old, he had seen plenty of unusual events in and around Cerknica town. Igor was a close follower of Monica. Every chance he had, he would climb the highest of the great fir trees and spy on the witch from afar. Now, there weren't any high-powered telescopes in those days but some worthy of the task. Sitting aloft, fifty feet above ground, Igor could see Monica's comings and goings quite easily; she always seemed to be wearing a black dress. *Maybe she had twenty of those dresses*, he would wonder. *But she sure looks beautiful and kind of scary just the same. I don't know whether to be afraid of her or in love with her. She sure is spooky, creepy woman.*

One day, as he sat high on his perch, he saw Monica looking up in his direction. He slid down a little lower on the branch as if to conceal himself like a strip of the black-colored bark. As he was sliding down the branch, his shirt, his favorite shirt, got caught on a sharp branch and cut the gray flannel material. His mother would be furious with him, he thought. "Damn it, I'll never learn. How will I explain this one?" As Monica continued to stare in his direction just as the situation seemed hopeless, a loud and thunderous noise directed the witch's attention. Someone had cut down one of the trees, and it struck the ground with a roar. *Thank God*, thought Igor. *Finally, I can get down from this tree.* Monica had wandered off to see what made that god-awful noise.

Yes, there were times when curiosity almost put him in harm's way. About an hour later, as Igor came to the edge of the clearing, he saw what looked like some type of religious symbol, a cross, standing there erect. As he got closer, his nostrils were assaulted by something that had a stench like nothing that he had ever experienced before.

"Something had been burned here, but what? Boy, did it smell." Igor ripped a small piece of his shirt. Igor folded his arm and covered his nose to conceal the smell and slowly inched closer. And closer still, his heart pounding in his chest, the silence was deafening! He thought he may be staring at someone's old scarecrow or something. Something that looked like a body but "How could that be?" His nose began to sting and itch so bad. He should at least find out what this thing is and get out of there. Barely two feet from the burning object, Igor let out a shriek that seemed to echo throughout the forest. So loud that some say it could be heard in Cerknica, more than two miles away. As he turned his head in disgust, he saw what looked like a white dress tied to a small juniper bush. *A dress that Monica would wear*, he thought. *A simple plain white frock*. At that instant, in that moment, he froze for what stood before him. It was the charred remains of a body. "Monica!" he screamed. They killed the witch. "Someone had killed my witch. They burned her on a cross and left her to die the most horrible of deaths."

Some say that burning to death is the most horrible way to die. The stench is overpowering and the reality most demoralizing to any observer. Igor could do nothing but stand frozen in his tracks and stare at Monica, the witch, the mysterious love of his life. "Why, why, why!" he screamed. "Who could do such a thing?" With that he scurried home to tell the tale of Monica the sorceress, burned at the stake. A tale that would be passed on throughout the ages, each a different version from the one before.

# 1974 CERKNICA

The young girl was running at top speed, incredibly fast, along the shoreline of Lake Bled. She seemed to lift off the ground, as if propelled by some mysterious and powerful force. So fast was she that some would say that she could outrun a dog or even, when some are exaggerating, a deer. Such an incredible athlete was Anastasia, and everyone knew it in the small well-kept town of Cerknica. Her full name was Anastasia Bohinj, but she preferred to be called Nasta for short. The boys in the neighborhood would jokingly call her Nasty and appropriately so. Anastasia had a wicked temper. She would blow up at the slightest provocation. Her eyes would bulge almost right out of her head, and her face would turn beet red. A scary sight indeed, especially for the young group of boys who were always chasing her and calling her names and throwing rocks at the young Slovenian girl.

Slovenia was a small country once part of Yugoslavia in the Balkan region of Europe, located next to Italy to the west, Hungry and Austria to the north. It had mountains and beautiful pristine lakes fed by the streams that run down from the mighty Alps. Anyone who travels there will marvel at its beauty and wonder why they had never traveled there before. Historically, Slovenia had been occupied by the Germans and Russians, to name a few, and adopted communist regime under the dictator Tito. But on this lonely spring day in April 1974, Anastasia Bohinj had nothing of those thoughts on her mind. She was running away from her would-be captors, those pain-in-the-ass boys from Cerknica town. Their names were Mitsa, Jacko, and Bogdan—three little piss-ants bothersome, arrogant kids. Their mission was to run down and capture the fox.

"I think she has run toward the mountain," cried Jacko, out of breath after having chased this girl for an hour straight. "Maybe we should quit and go home for now for it's starting to get dark, and my mother will surely punish me if I am late for dinner."

"No, no!" screamed Mitsa. "Let's keep chasing this clever one and be the first to ever capture her. When we do so, we will hold her down on the ground and tickle her with a feather. That will be fun. She'll be so angry, she'll start to cry."

"Let's be careful," said Bogdam, always the sensible one of the three. "She scares me with her temper. She's liable to beat us up."

"Don't be such a baby, little Bogdam. I am not afraid of any girl," said Jacko. "She doesn't scare me. She couldn't hurt me if she tried. Boys are always stronger than girls."

Anastasia Bohinj was twelve years old at the time, the daughter of Helena and Jacko Bohinj. Jacko was the only medical doctor within one hundred miles and knew just about everything there was to know about medicine. Helena Bohinj was a retired actress, living life vicariously as if still performing in a play some ten years ago. She was always the center of attention in a dark comedy.

The Bohinjes lived in a five-room cottage at the edge of central town, only a few miles away from Witches Mountain. Anastasia had two younger brothers, both with blond hair and striking blue eyes like their mother. But Anastasia was dark, like her father, with big brownish-green eyes like a doe, ever searching as if danger was always lurking. She was as good an athlete as any boy in town. She could easily outrun, outjump and outfight any of them. The fact is, most of the boys were afraid of her. She possessed a quick-witted charm that would capture anyone's heart, including the women of Cerknica. When Anastasia wanted something that caught her fancy, she often got it. She was envied and feared; this young Slovenian was somewhat of a legend at the ripe old age of twelve.

One day, a few years back, Anastasia was caught stealing in the local market. It was a hot day in the middle of the summer. Helena Bohinj had just taken an inventory of her refrigerator and decided she needed some food for dinner. People in Europe like to eat fresh food every day, so they shop daily. Leftovers are usually tossed away except in unusual circumstances. This day was no exception. "Nasta, Nasta!" screamed Helena Bohinj. "Where are you, my little cat? I need you to go to the market for me. Please hurry, it's nearing four p.m., and I need groceries."

"All right, Mother, be right there!" shouted Nasta as she answered the request of her mother. At the same moment, she sliced off the head of a captured bird with a kitchen knife. All in a day's play for Anastasia. She was constantly hunting and capturing animals for her pleasure. Some she would let go out of kindness and others she would swiftly and, with the precision of a surgeon, snuff out their lives. A coldhearted one indeed. "That will teach you, little bird. Don't mess around with this fox."

"I am growing impatient with you, young lady," cried Helena. "I am always on time for my plays and acting lessons. Punctuality is a virtue, my dear. Hurry."

Nasta was actually about two hundred yards away when she heard her mother. As quick as a tiger, with the grace of a cheetah, she darted off in the direction of her house, leaving the dead blue jay to be carted off by some carnivorous creature. She leaped over the fence at the edge of their property without breaking stride as if she were running an Olympic event she had once seen on the Bohinj's old black-and-white TV. Her stride was a joy to watch. An incredible athlete.

"All right, I am here, Mother. What would you like me to get at the market?" Even though she was angry for being interrupted from her hunting, Nasta spoke with the utmost politeness. She was a natural charmer. She believed you could get more with honey than arguing, and most of the time, she was right, especially with adults.

As she took the shopping list, she quickly thought of things she needed. Her razor-sharp mind was like a computer. Images of bubble gum, hair fasteners, chocolate candy, and a new hairbrush raced through her mind. Always concerned about herself, she was. "Me and me first" was her motto.

With list in hand, she dashed off to Magister's Market on the terrace de Fleur in the center of town. This particular market was known all over Slovenia. The owners had three stores: one here in Cerknica, one in Ljubljana, and one in the mountain town of Smyrna Gora. They ran a tight ship, and their shelves were always well stocked. Nasta sauntered down the aisle as if she owned the place.

"Hi, Mr. Magister, you look great today. Hello, Ms. Magister, your hair is lovely this afternoon."

As she bid her hellos, she was busy stealing her own supplies with the deftness of an experienced burglar. She always made sure she had lots of pockets on her pants when she went shopping. Nobody ever suspected this sweet young girl. This day was going to be different. A young store clerk called Mitja was watching Nasta as she hurried through the store. He happened to be in the back when Nasta came, and he could see her every move from up in the second floor lunchroom. Mitja's fascination with Nasta was no different than anyone else in town.

*She appears to be stuffing things in her pockets*, thought Mitja. *She's stealing. I knew she was a thief. I knew it. Finally, finally this little fox will get caught doing something wrong.*

He climbed down the old wooden stairs, looking to confront the girl. Mitja spotted her in aisle 3, the candy and pastries aisle, his favorite place in the whole store. As Mitja was about to tap Nasta on the shoulder, she suddenly turned around, as if she had eyes in the back of her head and confronted the boy. Her blue-green eyes stared at his as if she were looking right through him. A sudden feeling of impending danger overtook the boy. Her look was so evil that a warm, wet feeling began to trickle down his leg. Mitja composed himself.

"I caught you, Anastasia, I caught you stealing. I am going to tell the Magisters, and you will be punished. Hopefully, they will send you to the juvenile jail in Ljubljana."

Nasta was calm. "Mitja, my stupid and yet brave young man, if you do tell, I will become your mortal enemy, and that will never change. And remember this always," as she drew closer, she whispered in Mitja's ear, "revenge is a dish enjoyed most when it is cold." The boy's eyes bulged from their sockets as a puddle of warm yellow liquid formed under his feet. With that, Mitja flew out of the store, looking like he had just seen a ghost. Nasta began to laugh out loud, a high-pitched cackle, until her sides ached and ached. She loved the feeling of power so much that she even craved for it when it wasn't there. Like a chocoholic loves the taste and warm sensations that chocolate provides, Nasta liked power. She was born that way. Some innate sense that she possessed as if she was predestined to conquer something or someone.

*But what?* she would often wonder. *Why do I feel this way? Oh well. Back to being a young girl in the wilds of Slovenia.*

It was Easter Sunday, and everyone was dressed in their churchgoing best. Most of Slovenia practices Catholicism, and this holiday was no exception. The ladies wore the colors of the rainbow, having flowing dresses and, of course, the famous Easter bonnet that would dazzle even Pierre Cardin himself. All shapes and sizes, some with frills, others just plain and proper. The men were dressed in their Sunday best suits and sports coats. Although not a wealthy town, the men of Cerknica knew how to dress. They were instructed by their parents and their parents' parents that the clothes made the man. French-cut suits and lapels were common. Going to Paris, although a long and arduous task, was quite common. Many of the men in church, particularly the elders, also wore hats and fedoras that rivaled any. Anastasia and her family always liked to sit in the middle of the church. This way, they could view everyone who attended that day and critique everyone's attire. Helena giggled as the Munda family entered.

"Look at the dresses on those poor girls. They are the same ones they wore last year."

"Yes, Mother," Nasta replied. "Why don't you just leave them alone?"

"I cannot," replied Helena. "For I am a natural born critic and ardent lover of fine apparel."

"Oh, Mother, why don't you just say that their clothes suck and that you think you know everything about everything, why don't ya?"

"Because, Nasta, I am more refined that way, and someday hopefully, you will turn out just like me."

Nasta obediently nodded with approval just to shut

her up. But secretly, she despised her mother. A deep-seated hatred she developed years ago when she found out her mother had an affair with one of the local men from town. She was five years old, and one wintry snowy night, she was awakened by a crunching noise just outside her bedroom window. Her bedroom at the time was right next to her parent's bedroom. Her father was away at a medical convention in Austria—Strasbourg to be exact. So Nasta knew she was alone. When she heard the sound, she crawled across the wooden floor to the window and peered outside. There was a strong, gusty wind blowing, and there were two feet of snow on the ground. Nasta rubbed the sleep out of her eyes to see clearly, and there, crawling on all fours like a Saint Bernard, was old man Janko. He must have stepped on an old piece of wood, which would explain the crunching sound. He was a known boozer, so he was swaying as he stopped erect to tap on Helena's window. A midnight rendezvous for her mother, a clandestine meeting between the despicable woman who brought her into this world and the town's Casanova, a drunken one at that. *How long had this been going on?* thought the young Slovenian. That was a night that Anastasia would always remember, as she cried herself to sleep on that cold and blustery January night.

The church service finally ended, and Nasta was ready to go outside and confront the boys who always waited for her to appear. No different than any other Sunday, standing there with smirks on their faces were Jack, Milan, Bogdan, all waiting to get a glimpse at the one they called the fox, all dressed up in her Easter best. They couldn't believe nor cared to admit just how lovely she looked. Nasta was a beautiful young girl of twelve, and boy, did she know it. There wasn't a mirror in all of Cerknica that she was a stranger to. Every one she passed by, she would gaze into her reflection and nod with satisfaction. Nasta knew her beauty and was damn proud of it.

"If conceit were consumption, you would be dead, my dear," her mom would always say. "You are much too self-centered, young lady."

"But look at how those young wolves stare at me as they left the church, and look at them drooling at the mouth. If they could somehow have their way with me, even now, they surely would."

"Such blasphemous talk right outside a house of God. Shame on you, young lady. You should be punished."

Punished indeed. There wasn't a lock in all of Slovenia that Nasta couldn't pick. When she was seven years old, she met an old con man named Vlado Bernick. He was from the capital city, Ljubljana, population of three hundred thousand, a gaunt little European city with plenty of shops and restaurants. It even had a river running through it, just like every other city in Europe. But Ljubljana was also known for another element, a dwindling group of individuals called confidence men or con men. Grifters, gypsies who would no sooner steal all your money than smoke a cigar. Large groups of these people settled here years ago during one of the many wars that plague these parts. The city was a safe haven for drifters, those that chose not to fight. The decision was legal for these people because they were illegal aliens or wetbacks mostly from Hungary. They were issued green cards with temporary work visas. But instead of earning an honest living, they chose to steal and swindle instead.

Vlado Bernick had a heart. When he met Nasta at seven years, he was so impressed by her cunning and guile; he took her under his wing and taught her the game of life, with a shortcut. Nasta was eating pizza at the little Italian café in the town central. As she was munching and crunching her meal, she was enjoying it much so much she started squirming around, and some of her money dropped out of her pocket and hit the ground without a sound. Unbeknownst to her, Vlado Bernick saw this happen and actually heard the dinar hit the ground. Yes, believe it or not, the great cons can always hear money when it drops. Vlado slid his old worn oxfords on the floor over to the fallen money. He would purposely let a hole in the bottom of his shoe develop so he could actually slip his toes out of the shoe and grab the money without anyone seeing the theft take place. Nasta saw the whole thing coming; her instincts for one so young were truly amazing. And as Vlado drew his foot and the money within grabbing distance, Nasta suddenly and violently stomped on the old man's foot with her well-heeled school shoes. The girls in Catholic School were made to wear one style of shoe, and these happened to have large clunky thick rubber heels.

"Youuuuuuuu!" screamed Vlado. "Why in the hell did you do that?"

"Because I know your little game!" screamed Nasta. "I

saw what you did. You old thieves are all alike, but I am better than you. I am the fox. You set you up and boom, you got stomped." Laughing hysterically, Nasta was dancing around the café as proud as a peacock. She loved to dominate even at the age of seven. Something that was deeply ingrained in her, something that couldn't have been taught. As the ache in his toe began to subside, Vlado started to smile at the little prancing imp.

"You are good, young lady, the best I've ever seen. No one in these parts could ever hold a candle to you. Would you like to make some money with me?"

"Money? Sure, who wouldn't?" proclaimed Nasta. "But how could I possibly trust an old has-been thief like you, you old bag of shit!"

"Careful, little one, I am still quick with the knife. I'll slice off your fingers as quickly as you can say Ljubljana!"

"You don't scare me, old man," sneered Nasta. "Let's cut out all the junk and get down to the business of making money."

Bernick wondered to himself about just what and who he was getting into, but was so smitten by this young dynamo that he concluded, *Why not*? "Okay, young lady, you're on. Here's how we will get started. First . . ."

And so began the saga of the oddest couple of thieves in the history of Slovenia. Young Anastasia loved her new association with Vlado Bernick. Deep down inside, although she would never admit it, she came to love this generic Artful Dodger. He taught her every kind of scam imaginable. From the wallet in a string caper to pretending they were poor and destitute, hoping to get some type of monetary handout. Before long, some people got a little wise to their misguided adventures. The con game can be a dangerous one as the couple soon came to know.

It was Saturday in Ljubljana central, a beautiful day in June. When the weather was nice in this Baltic country, everyone would come out of their hibernation. This day was no exception; the streets were packed with locals and visitors alike. Every shop was open, displaying their wares. Unlike some other countries, the Slovenians are quiet and reserved people, even when it comes to making money and selling their products. They display a dour face and an occasional courteous smile. Old Bernick and the Little Fox were wandering down the main street, looking for some suckers, when they spotted an elderly couple, dressed very nicely, walking hand-in-hand on the other side of the street. They appeared to be alone and were content at that. They both had a twinkle in their wise old eyes as they would occasionally stop to kiss each other on the lips.

"Ahh, still in love," Bernick sighed to himself. "But more importantly, two good targets."

*The hunt begins*, thought young Nasta. *These two old geezers look like they were swimming in money by the way they are dressed.* The woman was wearing a chiffon dress, probably purchased in Paris, and the old man was clad in a Brioni suit with a gold Rolex President shining brilliantly on his wrist. They both walked upright, ever slowly, as if they owned the town. "Let's roust them," said Nasta. "You engage them in small talk, and I'll pick his pockets. We'll be out of eyesight before they knew what hit them. We'll go to Josef's Pub and have some pizza and mushrooms."

"Shut up for once in your life!" shouted Vlado. "Let me survey them a bit longer before we engage. Remember what I taught you. Be quick, but never in a hurry. You must learn to relax and stalk your prey deliberately."

*Sometimes the old man sounds more like an animal than a*

*human*, thought Nasta. But she knew that he was the master, for now anyway. Her time would come soon enough. Vlado approached the old couple with the stealth of a tiger and the grace of a British gentleman. He was wearing a recently stolen suit jacket and a pair of Nasta's father's borrowed trousers. He looked quite spiffy, for a gypsy that is.

"Excuse me, excuse me, sir, but did you happen to have dropped this by any chance?" Bernick held a coin in his hand and gave it to the couple. "I heard it drop on the pavement right by your fine shoes," lied Bernick. "Could it possibly be one of yours?"

With that the old man reached down into his pants pocket, the one that obviously held his money. This was Nasta's clue to move in closer to that side of his body.

"I am sorry, please allow me to introduce myself. I am Sir Issac Braxton from London," he lied in his best English accent. "And this is my lovely granddaughter Samantha. How do you do?"

"We are quite fine, thank you," replied the seniors at the same time. It was quite comical. "I am Carmella, and this is Rocco, we are from Naples, traveling through Slovenia on holiday. Isn't this such a lovely country?"

"Yes," replied Bernick. "We are enjoying it immensely."

As the conversation continued, Nasta found herself feeling left out, sort of ignored by her thinking even though the old gypsy was setting them up for the sting. With sweaty palms, Nasta started to reach for the money pocket when all of sudden, Vlado began to cough so loudly that she was startled for the moment and pulled back her hand right before it dipped down into the intending victim's pocket. *Shit*, thought Nasta. *What the heck is he doing?* As she caught Vlado wink his hazel-colored left eye, she now knew exactly what to do. Suddenly, as if it were rehearsed like a Broadway play, Vlado began to cough and this time retching violently, doubling over as if to vomit by the curb. Nasta shot her quick little hand in the direction of Rocco's money pocket as he bent down to help Bernick the thief. As her hand slid down this seemly endless crevice, her sweaty little fingers finally latched onto something that felt like paper. Money. Bingo. *Slide it out carefully, just like you were taught*, she thought. *And act cool and calm as you conceal it under your dress or in your bra.* As her hand began its ascent to freedom, she unrepentantly felt a vicelike grip on her hand

and immediately felt a searing pain up her arm. "Caught, oh my god!"

Nasta thought that her life was coming to an end. *How could this happen?* she wondered. *We rehearsed this a thousand and one times.* "Perfect execution" *were the words that Vlado used. It must work, I know it will.* Rocco continued to hold her wrist as tight as he could; after all, he is at an advanced age, and his strength was waning in his twilight years.

*This little bitch doesn't realize who f—— she is messing with here,* thought Rocco. *I have seen every little con game in existence. She thought she could get one over on me. No f—— way, you little whore.* "It is very possible that you could have pulled this little caper off on some ordinary run-of-the-mill fellow, my little woman, but not on somebody like me, you little piece of shit." As if by magic the old man's voice and mannerisms changed into the look of a tiger and the voice of Satan. "Do you have any idea who the *fuck* I am? You and your phony uncle or whoever he is were obvious from the get-go. I've seen every con there is, you fools. I saw this one from a mile away."

Rocco nodded to his wife for approval and a little empathy thrown in. He seemed to be embarrassed by his outburst in front of his wife because, in his world, respect meant everything to this man. Honor and respect were the themes of his world. This seemingly soft-spoken and docile elderly man was Rocco Reginello from Naples. He was a major player in the underworld in Europe. A gangster's gangster, he made his bones almost fifty years ago when he was an eighteen-year-old kid. He now was sixty-eight years old and set in his ways. Reginello had his hand in just about every racket known to mankind—from loan sharking to extortion, from drug running on the Isle of Sardinia to murder for hire. Rocco has done it all. That is precisely why he could travel anywhere in Europe and not fear for his life. He constantly was within eyesight and earshot of his big, burly, and dangerous bodyguards.

On this lovely spring day, Rocco and Carmella's shadows were Ino and Mario Monti, two well-known strong arms in the Reginello crime family. They were known to be vicious and cunning. They tipped off Rocco about the two scam artists as soon as they began their greedy little surveillance for any bad intent toward the old couple. Rocco was shielded from any bad intent, even from the gypsy con.

"What do you want me to do with you, little girl? I could

make you disappear with the snap of my fingers. As a matter of fact, do you see those two rather nasty-looking gentlemen across the street?"

"Ye-ye-ye-yes, sir," replied Nasta, shaking like a leaf.

"They work for me, and they no not like it when somebody tries to fuck with me and mine. In fact, they get very angry. Do you know what the f—— I am getting at?"

"Yes, sir," said Nasta.

With that, Rocco snapped his fingers, and the Monti brothers literally lifted old Bernick off his feet and guided him across the street and dropped him directly in front of their boss. Bernick looked petrified, and this normally olive-skinned man was now a lighter shade of pale. "Please spare us, señor. We didn't know who you were, we wouldn't have even tried to—" Bernick stopped in his tracks as Rocco lifted his index finger, waving it right next to old Bernick's nose.

"I don't want to hear your shit, old man. You're lucky that I don't have the two of you dumped in that river over there. Take your little con show and go somewhere else. If I ever see you near me or smell your rancid odor, I will order my men to escort you and your little wench to the bottom of the Adriatic permanently!" Rocco's voice was so deafening that it made Nasta literally sick to her stomach. She started retching and coughing so much that Rocco's wife bent down to comfort her. That was the last time that Nasta, the captured fox, and old Bernick ever tried to work the con in Ljubljana again.

# 1965 New Jersey

As the ball sailed over the left field fence, young Garrett LaPearl watched with delight as it cleared the railing by about twenty feet. He knew, by his young but powerful instincts, that the hit was a beauty and well-appreciated by the capacity crowd. He knew, as most of the great ones know, that he would be great in all his future endeavors, sports and otherwise. Players like Ty Cobb, Babe Ruth, Willie Mays, Roberto Clemente, and Maury Wills—they just simply knew that they were great. That feeling in the pit of the stomach an athlete gets to know when something significant happens. The eye of the tiger, call it what you want, or just plain old confidence.

Even at twelve years old, Garrett knew he was special. He could run faster, jump higher than any kid in town. A body of hardened sinewy muscle, Garrett was a young Adonis and conducted himself just that way for any sporting event. He was a crowd pleaser with a sense of style, a local hero to the people of Haddon Hills, New Jersey—a town of slightly more that ten thousand inhabitants, quiet by most standards with a bustling downtown area half a mile long. On any given summer night, there could be hundreds of people walking and shopping for that special gift or just simply watching the people watch each other. Haddon Hills was truly an ideal place to grow up. The schools were good educators, the streets were safe, and traffic always seemed to be minimal except on a holiday like July 4, when cars and people seemed to magically appear out of thin air.

Well, this August night was no exception. As usual, on Friday nights when the Little League teams were playing, a near-capacity crowd would gather to see their sons perform. Every now and then, a unique young girl would be on the roster, but it was very unusual for that year—1965. This night, Haddon Hills, undefeated at 15-0, was beating cross-town rival Audubon by the score of 13-3. Toward the end of the summer, neighboring towns would send their top players to different locations to compete all-stars. Haddon Hills was considered the cream of the crop, the top dog, as every team would try their best to beat them.

On this night, Garrett LaPearl slammed out four hits with two homeruns, pitched and struck out fourteen batters, and stole three bases. *Just another day at the office*, he thought to himself. Young Garrett did have one particular characteristic that wasn't so well received by his peers and adults as well. He sometimes had a red-hot temper that would suddenly, out of nowhere, flare up and breathe fiery flames on those that were present. Usually in life, this type of behavior came back to haunt someone or simply just fades away. When Garrett LaPearl didn't win the game or things didn't go his way, he would stomp his feet, spit out mucous, especially if he were pitching, knowing he would be the center of attention. But as those demons would suddenly depart, his friendly demeanor would draw people to him like a magnet. His father would always preach to him about being a poor loser. He would always say, "Nobody likes a poor loser, son. Nobody. Everyone wants to be close to the winner, Garrett, and sometimes even stand with the losing side. But being a poor loser with a hot-temper is not appreciated and not tolerated by anybody." Rocco LaPergio always seemed to know the right thing to say at the very precise moment.

Born to Italian immigrants, from the neighboring towns surrounding the city of Naples, Rocco was charming, clever, and extremely pleasing to the eye, especially from a woman's standpoint. They say he looked like Alan Ladd, the famous movie star. He carried himself with dignity and pride. With soft words, he could settle a dispute in just minutes without even raising his voice. Rocco was a man's man.

LaPergio family came to the USA via Ellis Island in 1909, the year of our Lord. They arrived with little to nothing and began the long and tedious task of becoming established in this immense, wild, and sometimes unfriendly land. Giuseppe and Carmella LaPergio were twenty-one and eighteen years old when they sailed into New York Harbor.

"Bella," cried Giuseppe. "Bella, my dream has finally come true. I have prayed and prayed that I should one day bring my family here. To start fresh, to start anew is a dream come true."

*I know I can make it here*, thought Joseph. *I just know we'll be all right.*

Carmella Risicci LaPergio was a beautiful raven-haired

young woman of eighteen years. She became a mother at age fifteen, not so uncommon in the early 1900s. She was wise beyond her years. With only a second-grade education, she was as streetwise as they came. Sometimes she even knew something was going to happen before it did. She was born in the province of Abruzzo in a small town called Milonico, in the hilly region surrounding Naples. Everyone was a farmer in this region for they didn't know any other ways to make money. Carmella's parents died when she was fourteen in a car wreck outside Rome. They were visiting relatives when their car was struck head on by a US military convoy truck. When the news reached Milonico, it was nearly a week later. Carmella and her seven brothers and sisters were devastated. Carmella knew she had to leave the place, or she would die at a very young age. She knew she would be thrust into a world that had no beginning and predictable end. Taking care of her siblings was acceptable to her, but her long-range intuition told her to pursue another direction, a new life someplace else. Carmella was one of only a few literate people in her town. Education not high on the priority list, she would read something every day in her spare time. Her days were long and uneventful. Her brothers and sisters were young and very needy. After a fifteen-hour day, Carmella was quite exhausted and mentally drained, but she possessed the inner strength and fortitude to pick up a book to read and learn. Underlining certain words was one of the little games that she played. "I would like to read and memorize a new word every day, every single solitary day."

One day, a very exciting event occurred. Carmella was in the local general store, located on the main street of her town, buying the necessities when she felt someone tapping her on the shoulder. It was old Cassini, the owner of the store. Carmella had a fondness for this gentle old soul. He always showed her the utmost respect. "Carmella, look what I have for you, my lovely young friend. This comes all the way from America, you know, the United States. It is a *Webster's Dictionary*, a word book. It has hundreds and hundreds of new words for you to know. It will keep you learning for the rest of your life. Take it, and go memorize some new words so you can use them in conversation with the townspeople. They will be so envious of your expansive vocabulary, you will be the talk of the town."

"I cannot accept this generous gift, Mr. Cassini, this book must have cost a fortune. You are a man of means, but this gift is too much. Please forgive me, I don't mean to be disrespectful nor ungrateful, but your act of kindness is overwhelming."

"Nonsense, señora, take this, or I will be very angry with you, young lady. Take it now." Mr. Cassini's voice was so loud and powerful that Carmella was stunned for a moment

"I guess I better accept your gift. Grazie. Grazie. You are so kind. I will never forget you, never!" She cradled the book in her arms as if it were a newborn child. The smile on her face stretched from ear to ear. At the young age of fourteen years, she truly felt like a twenty-one-year-old woman. This day would help her shape the rest of her life. Carmella knew she had better things in store for her, she just knew. Her doubts and fears were just like any other fourteen-year-old girl, but her courage knew no bounds. At that moment, she felt like she would do and say anything. The *Webster's Dictionary* would prove to be valuable to her future and one day become the cornerstone of her very existence. She didn't know then just how powerful command of the English language could be. Her first word in the new book that she chose just happened to be the word *passion*. Although she knew one meaning of the word and had used it on a number of occasions, it never occurred to her that the word was so versatile and, when used in the right context, would convey such strong ideas. Her passion for a better life was now set in motion. *What a special word*, she thought *I will use it for the rest of my life.*

Milonico Central was like something out of a western movie without the cowboys, gunslingers, and the Indians. It had a general store, or market as the Italians called it. The piazza as town square was where everyone would gather one time or another during the day or the evening. The bank or *banco* was the starkest-looking building. Although poverty was much too common, there were a few well-off people, and they deserved to keep their money kept safe for them.

In the province of Abuzzi, farming grapes for wine brought very good money for the times. The grape growers earned enough money to buy the best homes, cars, and the most land. Large tracts of land with rolling hills and grape vines as far as the eye would see were common there. *Truly a sight to behold*, thought young Giuseppe LaPergio, as he pedaled his old but sturdy bicycle in the outskirts of town. *I wish this old piece of shit would go faster*, he said to himself. *I'd be better off riding a donkey*, thought Giuseppe. *At least*

*I wouldn't have to pedal.* With that he began to laugh so hard that he fell off his bicycle right into a ditch by the side of the road. Luckily, he rolled on his shoulder upon impact and escaped serious injury. The ground was very soft and forgiving this time of year.

Harvest time, late May in Italia, is a great season to be anywhere in Italy. Not too hot and certainly not cold, the perfect Mediterranean climate. Italy is a gracious host to any traveler or inhabitant. The Lake District possesses some of the most beautiful lakes the eye can behold. The north region is often referred to as the Italian-Swiss region. Both languages are spoken freely, and some of the lifers are quite comfortable speaking both.

In the province of Abruzzo, life runs at quite a different and distinct pace. Young Carmella often believed that she would one day be found dead on the side of the road. "Death by boredom. I can just picture the headline in our stupid little paper—GIRL DIES BY DEATH BY BOREDOM." As she strode past the old Maggliani farm, she chuckled to herself and thought, *One day I will be out of this place. Please, God, help me please.* Suddenly Carmella spotted what looked like a body in an old drainage ditch by the side of the road. "Oh, dia mia, what the hell is it?" She quickened her pace until she stood directly over the corpse of the body or whatever it was. As she peered closer, the shape of a man was clearly what it was. "But who could this poor soul be? He must have had a bad tire on this bicycle," as she picked up the decrepit piece of aluminum. "He should have been riding a donkey, it would have been safer." She smiled. "This old thing has seen its last day on any road." She snorted aloud. Then, the prone body flinched, and suddenly his breathing was erratic. Coughing and sputtering, the body seemed to be coming alive like in Ms. Shelly's book *Frankenstein*. "I'll never forget that book," said Carmella. "It scared the Jesus out of me." With one good effort, the corpse came up to a sitting position. Mucous dripped from both nostrils and his hair was full of gravel. This part of Italy possessed both excellent topsoil good for farming and some sandy soil. He looked as though he had gray hair for seemingly such a young man, but upon closer examination, he had jet-black hair and beautiful green eyes. *I really don't recognize this boy*, thought Carmella. *But he is alive nonetheless.*

"Did I hear you calling my bicycle a piece of scrap? Do you realize that you have just insulted my grandfather, my father, and now me? This bicycle has been in our family for years!" shouted the corpse. "Who do you think you are, young lady? I mean, you are all of twelve years old. What do you know about fine traveling machines?"

"Not that much, boy," said Carmella. "But enough to know that I wouldn't be caught dead on this one. It's really a piece of *caca*." As the word rolled off her tongue and hit the airwaves, they both, at the very same moment, burst out laughing. They both laughed until their sides began to ache.

"You used that word like you owned it!" yelled Giuseppe. "Like you use it every day.

"Well, maybe I do, young man, just maybe I do. It's really none of your business."

"You are right, little woman, you are so right."

"Who cares that Joe, in English, was growing you know anyway." Insult after insult was exchanged, and both Carmella and young Giuseppe were starting to grow fond of each other, but neither would admit it. Their eyes finally met, and an awkward silence fell between them.

"Help me up," he barked.

"*Please* help me up," she said. "Say the magic word, and I will oblige."

"Okay, please, my fair maiden, please help me up, and I will be your friend for all eternity," he mused. "For the rest of your life and my life. In fact, I will never let you out of my sight."

The fourteen-year-old Carmella looked away and began to feel weak in her knees and a quivering in the pit of her stomach, something she had never experienced before. *Could it be that I am truly fond of this loud and obnoxious stranger? Could it be? Nah, I don't believe my own thoughts. I must be cracking up.* With that, her thoughts changed to her own safety and that of her newfound friend or whatever he was.

Now the once lifeless body began to dust himself off and stand tall. *Tall*, she thought. "Yeah, tall all right. That's because I am only five feet nothing," Carmella said loud. Once the stranger completed dusting himself off, upon closer examination, he didn't look all that bad, thought young and confused Carmella. He wore the latest craze in men's slacks, which were called bell-bottoms, which meant at the base of the trouser leg, the bottom had a bit of a flare to it, hence bell-bottoms. His were a rich wine or burgundy color, and he wore a typical, yet handsome, white buttoned-down oxford shirt. *He is rather dapper,* thought Carmella, *dapper indeed. I wonder if he can dance and if he likes children—lots and lots of kids running around everywhere. Is he handy with his hands, not for fondling girls' you-know-whats.* Most info young Carmella had about sex was from Mario's store and an occasional glimpse at *Time* or *Life* magazines. She was no different than other Brusseze girls in the early 1900s except that she had a burning desire to flee from here to see the world.

With dust flying everywhere, Giuseppe brushed off the last of it and immediately looked into the radiant staring eyes of Carmella. *For one so young, she truly was a sight. Her skin was pale yet radiant, an illustrious hue to it, after all, girls like her barely set foot out the door. She probably only goes out of the house when the sun is covered by clouds.* Giuseppe chuckled to himself. *Definitely not my kind of woman. She's too, too prissy. I'll wager to say that her hands don't have one callus or bump on them, and her feet are as soft as rose petals. Certainly not my kind of woman.* He sighed almost a sigh of disappointment. Because whether he cared to admit or not, young Joe, in English, was growing fonder of her by the minute or maybe it was by the second. The longer he stood and stared, the more he wanted to stay and chat awhile. But heaven forbid, he did not want her to know that; after all, she was only thirteen or maybe it was fourteen years young. *Too young for me*, he thought.

"What the hell are you gawking at, my fine dirty friend? Haven't you ever seen a girl before? And besides, I just don't like being stared at like I was some kind of object or animal or something!"

Throughout the ages, Italian men have been known to be somewhat chauvinistic and demeaning. They oftentimes possess not only a sharp nose but also a sharp tongue as well. Italian males really believe that a woman couldn't do all the work that a man could do, and Giuseppe was no exception.

Now Carmella began to feel very frigid and uncomfortable as she nervously began to shuffle her feet, swaying side to side as if she was controlled by a puppeteer. Her palms became moist, and she was sweating more and more, right through her newly darned socks.

*This guy I don't trust*, she thought almost loud enough to be heard or even partially deciphered by the young man. *He seems like the type that I see in the movie magazines. The kind of guys that speak fancy words, but really don't mean it, although he does have an honest-looking smile. And his eyes are kind and gentle. The eyes are the window to the soul, they say. I'll bet he doesn't even have a soul,* thought Carmella. As she went back and forth on what she truly felt about her first encounter with this older Giuseppe, Carmella felt like she did wish to see this guy again.

"Hey, señor, where do you live anyway? So you own your own home in town, or do you live on your trusty little bicycle? Tell me."

Giuseppe quickly became engulfed with the thought that maybe, just maybe, this young beauty actually liked him a little, *un petit. Now that couldn't be true. She thinks I am just a fool.* They both were overthinking the situation when in reality they were both falling in like with each other, although at fourteen years, Carmella was much too young to date. This young man, maybe not.

"Yes, señora. I do have a house that I reside in. The house of my parents near the old grist mill down by the lake."

Just as every other town in the region, a lake was present. All the lakes here in Southern Italy were fed by the clean, fresh water of the Mercure River, spectacularly crystal-clear water good enough to drink. People here did almost everything and anything influenced somehow by the lake.

"Oh, you live in the wealthy part of town." She sighed, and she almost seemed disappointed, as if to say "What would this guy want with a poor girl like me?"

"How would you like me to escort you home, young lady? It must be past your bedtime by now," he chuckled, as if to say to himself "This little person is probably as dumb as a fencepost with no education or book-learning. She wouldn't know what to do with a worldly guy like me anyway. I'm too good for her—too old and too good." Young Giuseppe felt as though he had some sort of power over the girl. *I must not try and take advantage of her. I would be the scourge of the town. People would hate me*, he thought.

The young girl blushed and nodded her head yes, not knowing why she did that. It appeared as though she was hypnotized. "Please, let's go now, señor. I must be home before it gets dark, or I will be punished by my father. He is very, very strict."

It was about 5:30 in the afternoon in the month of March, rather chilly for this time of year. As they walked along the stony pathway along the lake, they both were chatting away like they knew each other all their lives. They talked about religion and food, school and even money. They both concluded that money was extremely important and not to be abused. It was great to know that someone else felt the same as they did. Life was treating them good, for the moment. Carmella and Giuseppe were so smitten by each other they felt as though cloud nine was no longer a myth. That two people could actually be made for each other. Of course neither would verbalize this thought, but it was quite apparent to both.

As they approached Carmella's house, they both began to walk a little slower hoping to prolong the moment. Carmella lived on the outskirts of town; her house was quite modest, but very well kept. A white picket fence surrounded the house, giving it the appearance of a house you would see in a nursery rhyme—the proverbial ginger-bread house. Just as expected, Carmella's father was present on the porch, pacing back and forth with an anxious scowl on his face. Giuseppe felt something was growing in the pit of his stomach. His palms were sweating, and he was having a hard time breathing. "Boy, if this is what it would be like meeting my future father-in-law, I can surely wait awhile. This guy looks as though he wants to feed me to his dogs. I am only walking his daughter home to keep her out of harm's way."

Carmella's father, Michael, was a stern-looking, short, and rather round man of about forty-five years old. Olive-skin and a weather-beaten face, he looked as though he spent most of his life in the sun. *Being a farmer truly is not easy work*, he thought.

Carmella began to walk even slower now, slowing almost to a crawl. Young Giuseppe could tell that she was truly afraid of her father. "*Buona note*, Papa, so sorry I am a little late." It was now 5:50 p.m.; she was twenty minutes late. "I lost track of the time. I am so sorry," said Carmella. "Oh yes, this is my new acquaintance Giuseppe. He was kind enough to walk me home. Better than walking alone, don't you agree, Papa?"

"Si," said Michael, "but you are still late, and you will be punished. And I don't give a rat's ass who this young man is. Get in the house now, I mean, now." Michael's voice seemed to echo across the entire valley. Giuseppe was stunned; with that, he took off running, leaving Carmella standing there with her mouth wide open.

*Why, Papa, why? Sometimes you can be the cruelest person*

*in the world, I hate you. I hate you. Someday I will leave this place*, she thought. *One day, I will and never look back. My father expects me to be one of the nuns at the church, but no way, not me. I want to go to America and become a movie star. I even heard money grows there*, she said to herself. *I will truly die if I have to stay here much longer. I would rather die.*

Carmella's father was from the old-old school, the school that said women were beneath the man, and should be seen and not heard. He treated his wife, Carmella's mother Maria, like a slave. She was literally expected to cook, clean, take care of five children, and please her man in the process. Carmella watched this every day for the last fourteen years, her entire sweet, short life. No way would any man treat her this way. She instinctively knew that one could always get more and that cooperation was the main ingredient in any relationship. Even though until now she had never even been with a man, boy, or whatever, she had the self-confidence that her future marriage would be different than her parents'.

# NASTA GOES TO ENGLAND (AGE SIXTEEN)

It was 1972, and rock-and-roll songs were blasting on the radio everywhere. As Nasta walked off the plane, she wondered to herself how she ever got talked into coming to London, England, to attend secondary school. Having never flown before, she was amazed at how large an airport Heathrow was. "Cerknica would fit over there," she chuckled to herself. "This place is huge."

At sixteen, Nasta was absolutely stunning. Her hair was now long and obviously well kept. As a young girl in Cerknica, she preferred her hair cut short as if to look like one of their other boys who chased her every day of her life. She ambled down the portable stairway onto the tarmac, looking foolishly for familiar faces. *I don't even know anyone in this country. I must be losing my mind*, she thought. *All*

*I know is that England is definitely not Slovenia. Where the fuck am I, and why did I agree to this?* Nasta had agreed at the request of her mother to attend secondary school in London when she was just ten years old. Her mother even made her sign a contract, binding her in writing to the agreement. *People here look as though they are stiff or something*, she thought. *Like they have a piece of wood stuck down their pants supporting their back, thus keeping their shoulders ramrod straight. Very proper indeed*, she thought. Nasta chuckled as she said that statement aloud because she just heard someone else say it on the plane, having never heard it before.

Nasta read many, many books as a young girl in Slovenia, mostly at the request of her father, a well-read man himself. She liked to read about other faraway countries; one in particular was England. It always struck her as a place she might like to visit. So when the opportunity to go was presented to her by her family, she jumped at the chance. "England? Me in England? That would be the greatest," she whispered to herself. The thought of her being proper and speaking the King's English almost made her shudder and laugh aloud at the same time. "I am the fox," she said to herself. "Nothing will ever change that. I can outrun, outthink any man from any country. I will accept this challenge presented to me, chew it up, and spit it out. London town, make way for the new and cultured fox." With that thought, she burst into a raucous laugh, turning the heads of some people in the airport standing close to her.

Standing there in the airport terminal, everyone seemed like they were in a hurry in this country, observed Nasta. "Going this way and that, but where the hell were they going?" she wondered aloud. *It is two in the afternoon, why aren't they at their jobs?* she thought. *And why doesn't everyone carry a suitcase or overnight bag?* she thought. Truthfully, Nasta had never been in an airport before, only to train and bus stations. She didn't know that many people were waiting for their luggage to come out of the carousel.

She also didn't know that a pair of sinister yet friendly eyes was following her every movement. The eyes were looking for outstanding character traits, how she walked, and how she handled herself in a crowd. *Is she the right one?* thought the stranger with the bright blue roving eyes. *Did they make a mistake with this one? The one from the tiny, little known country of Slovenia? The one they called the fox?*

*She appears rather fidgety. Somewhat nervous type of girl,* thought the stranger. *Perhaps she is simply homesick already, missing her loved ones back in her country. After all this lass called Anastasia flew here alone with no supervision, what could I expect?* thought the one with the well-trained eyes. The stranger was indeed no stranger to this type of situation. He in fact has seen and done this type of work many, many times before. These eyes belonged to one Nigel Brighton.

Nigel was a proper British gentleman, living in a posh neighborhood just outside of London town. His family consisted of wife Margaret, one son Alex, and a daughter Isabel. Simple people living a simple common life in jolly old England. Nigel was tall and quite trim for a chap of fifty-two years. He kept in shape lifting weights, swimming twice a week, and playing lots of tennis. His appearance with his Burberry topcoat gave him a look of affluence and style. This day, he left his family at home, deciding to gather Nasta alone and bring her back to the house. The Brightons were a host family, strict educators, accepting the job of keeping this young Slovene at their residence as a foreign exchange student. Nasta Bohinj would be staying with the Brightons for approximately six months.

Nigel continued to watch her from afar for another fifteen minutes. He really didn't want to wait too much longer to introduce himself for the fear of her becoming scared and uncomfortable in this foreign country. Nigel zeroed in on the girl and began to slowly walk toward her. She was wearing blue jeans, a bright yellow blouse, and black boots. As Nigel approached, she had turned her back in Nigel's direction, and with that, he tapped on her shoulder.

"I say, are you Anastasia Bo-bo," he stumbled purposely, trying to pronounce her surname, for he knew exactly how to pronounce this name. It was all in her files. Just as Nigel was about to speak again, Nasta had whipped around and almost knocked Nigel over with her hands clenched in a fist.

"Don't ever sneak up on me like that again!" shouted the girl. "You scared the heck out of me, and besides, you could have been hurt. You really don't look much like you can fight or anything. I am sorry, and here is your handkerchief that you dropped," she said as she bent down to retrieve it for him.

"My dear girl, I am Nigel Brighton, your host father for the next six months. I am here to take you to your new home here in England. I am sure that your mother received the paperwork in the mail."

"Indeed," giggled Nasta, "but I think I didn't read the goddamn stuff my mother did. She took care of everything, so I don't know nothing."

"Young lady, it really is unnecessary for you to use profanity, and the proper English is I didn't know anything."

"Well, I stand corrected then, Sir Nigel. I can see me and you are going to get along famously."

"You and I," said Nigel.

"What?" said Nasta.

"You and *I*," countered Nigel.

"I know how we go with the proper shit again."

The ride to the Brighton house was rather quiet. Nasta was weary from her day of travel and anxious to unpack and see her new residence in England. She was picked up in a brand-new Mercedes, the color of silver with black interior. Never before had she rode in such a fine vehicle. *This car seems to have a mind of its own. Gadgets, buttons, and all sorts of contraptions*, thought Nasta. *I never thought I'd be treated like this.* This car even had windows that went up and down with the push of a button. Nasta was in heaven. When the sleek Mercedes pulled up in front of a large house surrounded by an iron fence, Nasta was beside herself. *I hope to have a ball here.* The house referring to an old, old English Tudor, large with a well-kept lawn that she could see from the car. *These people must be loaded*, thought the young fox. *They are friggen loaded.* She had adopted some American slang, *friggen*, from watching TV at home. *Yes, England was looking pretty good so far. I cannot believe that me, Nasta Bohinj, could have this opportunity and for what? Being me.* For a brief moment, her blood seemed to be running both hot and cold. If she had any hair on the back of her neck, it would have been standing straight up in the air. Something is odd about this whole arrangement.

It started when she was in the seventh grade in her hometown of Cerknica. A letter arrived one day containing an advertisement for the recruitment of the smartest and most well-rounded young ladies in Slovenia. Nasta never had the opportunity to read the letter, but allegedly, it included a trip to England as an academic exchange student with all expenses paid for a two-year period. *Surely there are smarter and more talented girls than me*, she thought. The letter was addressed to the Bohinj family with Nasta's name in bold letters. It arrived on a school night, and she didn't notice the letter until about 9:00 p.m. on a Tuesday. Right about when she was going to bed.

"What was that letter all about, Mother? It has my name on it. Does it contain any money?" asked Nasta.

"Oh no, you are not going to pry information out of me by being clever," said her mother. "You just close your eyes and go night-night." Something her mother always said to her throughout out her childhood. "Please, I will tell you in the morning. I do not want to ruin the surprise."

When Nasta awoke the next morning, her mother read the letter to everyone in the family while they ate their breakfast of different Slovenia breads and home prepared jellies and jams. The Balkan countries were famous for their breads, especially Slovenia.

As Nasta lay on a beautiful Victorian featherbed, a poster bed at that, she drifted back in time and recalled the morning two years ago when she was told she was going to England to further her education. Nasta Bohinj was to become a foreign exchange student for two years in England. Lying on her back, staring up at the ceiling in this lovely and charming

English Tudor, Nasta thought aloud, "Wow, I really live here in England. Me, a nobody from Cerknica, staying in this mansion. Holy shit, it is really happening."

Her room in the Brighton house was quite large and so finely decorated. All her favorite colors in the expensive wallpaper. "Almost as though they knew my tastes and favorite things. A stuffed dog like my dog at home. I mean, that is too coincidental. How did they know? Unless, of course, my mother told them. They even have my favorite gumballs in a bowl over there," she said. "This place is too much!" Nasta's thoughts were interrupted by a loud knock at the door.

"Ms. Anastasia, Ms. Anastasia, are you awake?" The voice on the other side of the door was sweet and refreshing. The kind of voice that makes you feel comfortable immediately. The voice of an angel.

"Come in," said Nasta. "Please come in."

Margaret Brighton entered the room, and immediately, her beautiful blue eyes stared at you as if she knew you all her life. They were so big and so blue. It was like looking into crystal-clear water of the Caribbean Sea. They were the most beautiful eyes she had ever seen. *She is gorgeous.*

"How are you doing in your new surroundings, young lady?" asked Margaret. "Did you enjoy the limo ride from the airport, Anastasia?" inquired Margaret.

"Please call me Nasta, Mrs. Brighton. I absolutely hate my proper name."

"Very well, I shall call you Nasta if you call me Margaret. After all, we'll be spending quite a bit of time together. We might as well be comfortable with each other."

*What does she mean by that?* thought Nasta. *I guess she means in the classroom probably.*

"For the remainder of the day we will be touring the estate to familiarize you with this place, especially the classrooms and laboratories where you will be studying biology and various medical subjects. When you are through with us, you will be just this side of a doctor," explained Margaret.

The Brighton estate covered about twenty acres of wooded area with beautifully manicured lawns and a number of old buildings. It almost resembled prison. One of the buildings housed the laboratories and even an old gymnasium, something like the ones in Slovenia. An old gym, but when Nasta took a tour to see the facilities, the gym had all types of the latest exercise equipment. Anything from free weights, stationary bicycles, a sizeable swimming pool to something Margaret referred to as Nautilus equipment.

*It was truly amazing,* thought Nasta. *I will be built like a Greek goddess when I am finished here. I can't wait.* Nasta's thoughts were interrupted when Margaret spoke about exercise.

"A sound body creates a sound mind, young lady. You will be expected in the gym every single day. Yes, that's right, seven days a week. Some part of exercise will be part of your day. We think you will enjoy and appreciate our methods. If one takes good care of their body, with a healthy diet and a daily exercise routine, the mind can greatly benefit from it," explained Margaret. "Come over here, young lady, and allow me to introduce you to the latest equipment. The year 1977 has brought us many new advancements to the world of fitness. We truly believe that these advancements are only the beginning of a possible million-dollar industry. We like to stay on the cutting edge of everything from fitness to a state-of-the-art library over on the other side of the estate."

*This lady is unbelievable,* thought Nasta. *Does she ever shut the heck up? But there is something about her that I like. She has softness. She is rather beautiful at that.*

Margaret Richardson Brighton was indeed quite beautiful by most standards. She possessed a striking countenance with an almost patrician-like nose. With shoulder-length tawny-colored hair, she had lovely high cheek bones, the perfect facial structure. She was a model in New York for ten years before marrying Nigel. She had bright blue eyes that were so piercing that one could easily become hypnotized by them. She stood five feet eight inches tall in her bare feet. Her finger and toenails were perfectly manicured; she possessed the longest of fingers and perfectly shaped feet. She also, for a short time, had become a hand model in her younger years. Yes, Margaret was quite stunning, almost beyond belief.

"This is called Nautilus, the latest equipment for toning and shaping. It also makes you very strong. We believe—"

"Yeah, I know, strong mind, strong body," reiterated Nasta.

"Please do not—" Margaret's face became contorted and looked something like a gargoyle, thought Nasta. She suddenly lost her kind-looking face and snarled. "Please, please do not ever interrupt me again. Ever! I despise that in anyone, not just you, my dear Nasta." Just then her rage subsided, and she became cool and calm again.

*Wow, this chick is a real loose cannon*, Nasta thought to herself. *Maybe she's having her period. She always seems as though she is looking right through me and right out my asshole.* Nasta smiles for a brief moment and caught Margaret's eye.

"Wipe that stupid smirk off your face, young lady, and continue listening to what I have to say!" shouted Margaret. "If you fail any of your courses or receive an unsatisfactory grade, you will be dismissed from this school. Do you hear me?"

"Yes," replied Nasta. "I will behave, Mrs. Brighton. I know you do not like me, and I will keep my smiles and comments to myself. Because if I—"

"Please close your mouth, my dear, and do not say a word!" said Margaret. "I repeat, do not say a bloody word."

At that moment, a tall, lean, extremely fit young man walked into the room. He was about five feet ten inches of lean hardened muscle. In fact, his entire body, including his head, appeared to be made of muscle. He walked up to Nasta and Margaret and introduced himself as Gunther Zell. "I am your personal trainer, Ms. Anastasia Bohinj. I will see you every day for approximately two hours and a half. We will train for fitness, which will include dexterity, flexibility, good health and hygiene, use of weaponry, and various other forms of fitness. You will not question anything I tell you in the beginning of your regimen, but after six weeks, you will be allowed to ask questions and hopefully feel more comfortable with your surroundings."

Nasta thought, *Weaponry? Why and what is he talking about? If he meant guns, they were the farthest things from her mind.*

"Please proceed, Heir Gunther," said Mrs. Brighton. "I trust you will work her very hard and yet be gentle and fair with her. After all, she is our star pupil." Gunther Zell merely nodded at Margaret's statement as if there was some deep secret agenda going on here. A plot.

"Ms. Anastasia, please remove your shoes and socks, and come over to the mat before you. Do not lie down, just stand there!"

"Please call me Nasta. I'd feel much better."

"Silence, young lady," barked Zell. "Remember what I told you before. Speak only at the proper time."

"And when would that be, Gunther?" inquired Nasta.

"When I tell you it is all right to speak," replied Gunther.

"Only then. Now please be quiet and pay attention! Flexibility is a very essential ingredient to good health. If your body is lean and lithe, you will move more gracefully and think more clearly. The ancient practice of Yoga will be excellent to start the process."

Nasta had heard of it, but never indulged in such a routine as she was about to learn. She was simply used to running and climbing back in Cerknica. She was always running away from some young male seeking to capture and torture her. But she was just too fast.

"Please stand as straight as you can, Nasta, feet together, and without bending your knees, gently and slowly try to touch the floor with your palms." Nasta had painted her finger and toenails black, which looked quite unusual, and she could only lower down where her palms were still about five inches from the ground.

"This is as far as I go," said Nasta. "I can't go any further."

"Nonsense, young lady, when I get done with you, you'll be putting your chin to the ground!" yelled Gunther. "Now straighten your back, take a deep breath through your nose, and as you lower down once again, let all the air out through your mouth and slowly lower to the floor."

This time, Nasta got much closer to touching the floor than before. "You are good, Heir Zell, damn good," quipped Nasta. "I feel more flexible already."

"Next I will ask you to stand with your feet a couple of inches apart, bend one knee up, and grab the bottom of your foot with both hands and lift your leg upward. After that, attempt to straighten the leg until it is fully extended and parallel to the floor, and hold that pose for ten seconds."

"I don't think any word a swami, this is definitely a challenge, even for someone as graceful as myself, Heir Gunther. What are you trying to do here anyway?" asked Nasta. "Am I secretly training to be a ballerina or some dancer of sorts?"

"Not quite, Ms. Anastasia," replied Heir Gunther. "Yoga enhances and expands the mind, after all, that is why you came here in the first place, isn't it?"

Nasta thought to herself, *This guy is really creepy, and he never looks me directly in the eyes. It's as if he has some other agenda. He is a weirdo,* she concluded. *A plain old weirdo. At times, I feel as though this place has something else going on. Something completely different than plain old academia. I just don't know what it is yet,* thought Nasta. *But I will figure it out, I am sure of it. Unless of course, it is merely my imagination.*

# 1976 NEW JERSEY

Garrett LaPearl sauntered down the main street of Haddon Hills this day with an extra bounce in his step, for he had just recently learned he was chosen to be an all-star in basketball for the state of New Jersey. This was an honor he had passionately longed for and tediously worked for the last four years. Garrett had been a star baseball player all through his childhood but had become smitten with basketball in the eighth grade. There was a young Catholic priest with extensive knowledge of the game and a burning passion to teach young boys the fundamentals of the game. His name was Father Conner Jackson. Father Jackson came from a poor county of Tipperary, Ireland. His parents were pig and sheep farmers as they owned and cared for a fifty-acre plot of land just south of the city of Donegal, not far from the coast. Conner Jackson loved his life just like any other young Irish lad. Playing long hours in the beautiful green fields and coming home exhausted when the sun began to set. He lived to be outdoors, to smell the sweet smell of the flowers, and to roll in the thick green emerald grass. Conner Jackson enjoyed every single day.

"I just want to be an altar boy ma," said Conner. "I want to be more involved in me church."

"*My* church, not *me*, speak the proper English, lad. The King's English," said Mary Jackson, formerly Mary Ryan from County Cork. "Say *my* church. Don't acquire my bad habits."

"Yes, Ma," spoke Conner. "If you say so."

"Well, be what it may, go on and join the group of altar boys and do right by our Lord. Remember do everything you love with great passion, and you will be truly happy in your life."

Conner would later become Father Jackson, a Catholic priest. And so Conner Jackson of County Tipperary began his journey into the realms of Catholicism and would someday, hopefully, travel to the United States and lead a long and devoted life.

*All-state*, thought Garret, *this is just unbelievable*. Jimmy

Anderson, a pint-sized but sturdy second guard on Garret's team was the first to learn of Garrett, his best friend's good fortune.

"Yo, Gar, you are definitely a king, my friend. I knew it right from the beginning, the first time I saw you play. I knew you had it. I knew you would be a great player. And I was right as usual. It helps being the boy brains of the class," laughed Jim. "I didn't get straight As for nothing."

The girl brain of the class was Carrie Nyson. She lived over on Walnut Terrace and was best friends with Garrett and Jimmy. She too learned of Garrett's newly acquired honor and called him immediately.

"I can't wait to tell my father," said Garrett. "He will be so freakin' proud of me. I can't wait to tell him. He always said that one day I could be a champion if I worked hard. Well, damn it, he was right. But all-state. I figured all southern Jersey, not all-state."

The team that Jimmy and Garrett played on finished with a 33–0 record, the first time in the state's history that any high school team went undefeated. At that moment, the phone in Garrett's house began to buzz. "It's probably the press," joked Garrett. "They probably want to interview me and who knows maybe even you"—referring to Jim—"you little twerp." Garrett picked up the phone. Carrie Nyson was on the other end.

"Hey, how's it going, Mr. All-state Basketball? The love of your life is standing right here, dying to talk to you."

"Well, who may that be?" joked Garrett. Carol Ann Dermott laughed with such intensity she nearly began to hyperventilate. "Be cool, man, you are as they say, definitely a king." Jim, Carol, Carrie, and Garrett continued their congratulatory moment when the phone began to ring once again.

"Answer that, Jim. I don't feel like being color-drained out of this face." He couldn't speak; he just stood there stammering. "Spit it out!" yelled LaPearl. "Who the frig is on the other end? President Kennedy's ghost?" With that, Garrett seized the phone from his friend and questioned the caller. "This is Garrett, who's this?"

"Garrett LaPearl, son of Rocco."

"Why, yes."

"I am afraid I have some bad news for you, young man. Your father has been gunned down on Broad Street in the City at two this afternoon."

"Oh my god, oh my god!" screamed Garrett. "My father has been killed. My father was shot to death."

Tears streamed down LaPearl's face like raindrops from monsoons in Asia. Garrett kneeled down and wept uncontrollably. Jimmy, Carol, and Carrie just stood there and stared. Little did Garrett know then, this was a very cruel lie staged by a faceless enemy.

Rocco LaPearl was a man of the streets, growing up in Philadelphia and the city across the river, Camden, New Jersey. Although a small city on the waterfront, Camden was known for its fine restaurants and great entertainment. It was also famous for its underworld activities and ties to organized crime. Rocco, or Rocky as he was known on the streets, was a member of the local mafia clan started long ago by the local Don or Padrone Marco Ginelli. Rocco LaPearl came up through the ranks very quickly and without a whole lot of fanfare. His real name was LaPergio, later shortened to a more Americanized name like LaPearl. Rocco was quiet and extremely handsome. He resembled the great actor Alan Ladd and was very at-home with the female persuasion. When Rocco walked down the street usually clad in a custom-made suit by Dom's Tailors, the girls would line up to get a better look. Rocky knew the young city girls were off limits to the gangsters as he was familiar with the punishment on those who ignored the laws of the mob. Resting atop his perfectly cut hair was usually a fedora, the latest style, which he would graciously tip when he passed a curious onlooker. Rocco knew how to charm the ladies. It wasn't unusual for him to escort the woman across the street and keep them out of harm's way. He flirted, but never touched the locals. At home was his wife of twenty years, Fiona, and his young sons Garrett and Joseph. Usually the gangsters kept mistresses stashed away somewhere in the city. Paying for their apartments and escorting them to shows across the river in Philadelphia and occasionally in New York. Rocco's life was good and very lucrative.

The chain of command in the Ginelli family was no different than any other mob family all over the United States and Italy. The Don was on top; next the underboss; the consigliere, personal counsel to the godfather; the *capo* or captains; and the foot soldiers. They were called made guys or wiseguys.

Each and every made guy had to do a piece of work or participate in a murder of an enemy and therefore get his badge and enjoy the privilege of being a member of the mafia. Rocco was no exception. He did his piece of work fifteen years ago when he was instructed to take out Blackie Bean's kid brother for selling drugs. As much as Rocco detested violence, he had no choice. He put two behind the kid's ear one wintry night over on Royden Street and that was that.

Rocco LaPearl said very little about his comings and goings because he strongly felt that what they didn't know about wouldn't hurt them. Fiona took care of the house and also chose to pursue a college degree. Rocky was a little different than most mobsters in that he allowed such endeavors. Fiona was strong and quick witted. *She deserved to better herself,* he thought. "What class are you doing tonight?" he would ask. "I hope it has something to do with romance, not that we need to improve in that category." He chuckled. "After all, we still do it two times a week and sometimes more, don't we, honey?" Rocco and Fiona were still hopeless romantics even after twenty years of marriage.

Rocco's other son Joseph was born to be a lawyer. From his early days in school, Joseph did very well. Unlike Garrett, sports was important but not the be-all and end-all. He and Garrett were close, but very different people and respected each other immensely. Both boys were handsome like their father and very compassionate and kind like their mother. "A great combination of looks and brains," Rocco would often say.

That fated day was one of the most beautiful spring days that one could ever imagine. The state of New Jersey has its flowers, as most Jerseyites would agree, when the trees are in full bloom and the sky was bluer than a pair of old faded jeans. New Jersey could be quite lovely. The city of Camden was what you call an industrial city, blue collar all the way. Unions were thriving, unemployment was low, and for the most part the economy was strong. The gangsters kept a sharp eye on the economy, especially their own. You see, the mafia has its own economy to look after. Theirs is different than the norm, more like a subeconomy and underground flow of capital that you couldn't read about in the city or local paper, *The Daily Post*. Lone sharking, gambling, prostitution, shakedowns, etc., were the main sources of income for the mob. Occasionally, someone has to be killed or whacked to maintain the balance, or even peace for that matter.

Rocco LaPearl had no idea that he was being hunted by a sinister and deadly character. When Rocco finished his business in the city, he would jump into his Cadillac and ride back to Haddon Hills about five miles away. He decided to move out of the city when Garrett and Joseph were young so they wouldn't get caught up running the mean streets and maybe one day recruited by the mob.

On this day, Rocco was anxious to get home, shower, shave, and get over to the gym to see his son Garrett play basketball at the local high school in the spring league. Rocco parked his vehicle on High Street and proceeded to walk the half block that led to the gym. As he got out of the car, Rocco suddenly felt uneasy, like a tiger sensing someone or something was watching him. A gangster's world is a world of perception, quick decisions, and staying alive. He looked around with his gray green eyes and quickly concluded that it was nothing and that he should get to the game before they started. He liked to get there a little early so he could talk to his son before they started. Even though he never played the game, he always gave good advice. This game was not an exception. Rocco was quite wise.

"Stay calm out there, son, don't get nervous."

"Oh, I won't, Pops. I'll probably hit my first shot."

"If conceit were consumption, you would be dead," Rocco

said with a smile. He got that little ditty from his wife. She had a million of them. "And be a good sport out there!" yelled Rocco as the players took the hardwood.

The buzzer sounded, and the players began their magical dance. Up and down, up and down they ran. *It was almost like watching a ballet,* thought Fiona until she heard young Jimmy Anderson curse after he missed a layup, but Fiona knew that was all part of the game. Garrett ended up scoring 24 points and gave out 8 assists. Of course, Carol Dermott and Carrie Nyson were at the game, watching their heartthrobs play. Rocco felt a bit uneasy throughout the entire game, and his nervousness was not apparent to anyone else to take notice. *Oh well, just paranoia, I guess, a gangster's best friend,* he thought. But he chose to call it simply being cautious.

Sam Sillento was a member of the LaPearl family. Her mother and Fiona were sisters and lived in Haddon Hills as well. Sam was thirteen years old, reed thin, and very funny, with lots of energy. Her light brown hair was cut short, almost like a boy, and her huge blue eyes were always wide open. Some of the neighborhood kids would tease her, but Sam just shrugged it off and continued her walk to the gym to see her favorite cousin Garrett play basketball.

She didn't notice a pair of black sinister eyes watching her through a large thicket on the corner of Ninth and High Streets. Those eyes belonged to one Blackie Colombo, a well-known enforcer for the mob based in Philadelphia. Rocco LaPearl's family based in Camden was an extension of the Philadelphia family, also under the guise of Marco Ginelli, the boss of bosses. Blackie Colombo was a made guy, known for his quick temper and use of the garrote, a seldom-used device to kill people at close range. The killer needed to be directly behind the intended victim in order to wrap this device around the victim's neck, particularly the larynx. Once the garrote was in place, the killer will then tighten the rope and crush the larynx and immediately kill his victim. A very uncommon weapon for a hired hit, but effective just the same. Blackie was good with it and highly experienced. Blackie was believed to have about 30–40 notches on his belt, possibly earning the distinct title of mass murderer. Blackie worked exclusively for the Ginelli family and, in the past month too, the contact for the popular Rocco LaPearl.

When the Ginelli family counsel met, they particularly and specifically discussed the future hit on LaPearl. Don Ginelli spoke very slowly and deliberately.

"He is a terrific wage earner, loyal through and through. He is not flashy and keeps a very low profile in the newspaper. He's never skimmed anything that we know of, and he gets a lot of respect from his crew. Then why whack him?" Washtubs asked. Washtubs Ginelli was a local leg-breaker and warlord cousin to Don Ginelli. He is permitted to sit at the counsel. Though only a foot soldier, he has respect because of his family connections.

"Because he is too good," bellowed the Don. "Goddamn good." At the end of the sentence, the Don started to cough and choke violently, and everyone in the room just stood there and watched until the retching ceased. "Oh dear mia," he said. "Please let us continue." The Don's face was beet red and his forehead riddled with beads of sweat glistening from the light of the Tiffany lamp. "He is so good that one day—listen to me—one day he will wake up and decide that he should be the boss, and bada bing bada bing, you have a new leader. This man is very cunning do not let your guard down with him."

Some of the other counsel members were in total disagreement with the Don, but they would be goners if they showed their true feelings.

"I am sixty years old," spoke Ginelli. "I still have many good years ahead of me. LaPearl is young and strong, very popular with everyone. He has got to go. Now." Normally, they don't make somebody "go away" because of potential threat, but no one was about to question the Don. "I will put Blackie on this one, and we will pay thirty thousand dollars, a fair price, don't you all agree?"

Right on cue, as if they were all rehearsed previously, they all nodded their heads in approval. "Very well, gentlemen, it is done. The hit has been approved, and may God bless your souls and the souls of our enemies."

Rocco was watching his son being received by his adoring fans when suddenly that feeling of paranoia reared its ugly head. Rocco's eyes were wide open and scanning the room for a hint of unordinary behavior or someone who really looked like they didn't belong. *Better to be safe than sorry*, he thought. Who would try something in a crowded high school gym? Garrett, circled by well-wishers, spotted his father about to skip out of the side entrance when he called out his name.

"Yo, Pops, I told you that I would make my first shot."

"It was a layup, son," laughed LaPearl, "but a great one just the same."

"Thanks, Pops, for coming to the game."

Garrett always showed his respect by being appreciative of his father's attendance. Of course, his mother was no exception. She came running over and was quickly embraced by her son and her husband.

"Excellent game, Garrett, you were very good out there."

"Thanks, Mom. I couldn't have done it without you. Well, I have to get back to the house and study," said Fiona.

"And I must go and be with my adoring fans," laughed Garrett. "I'll see you guys back at the house. Hey, there's cousin Sam, my biggest fan. She'll probably ask for my autograph," joked Garrett.

"I must go." Rocco stood and watched as his family dispersed in different directions. The side door exits were close as Rocco pushed the side bar and the doors flung open. It was a beautiful moonlit night in November, and a harvest moon was displaying its natural flashlight-like power in his quaint little New Jersey town. Blackie lay in wait about half a block away in a clump of bushes and sassafras trees on

High Street. He had been watching LaPearl for about three weeks, trying to establish his patterns upon leaving the gym. Being a wiseguy, Rocco always tried to vary his departure and not be too predictable. This night was no exception. He slipped out the side school exit, took the longer route to his car parked on Walnut, and headed to his white Cadillac. Every gangster dreamed of owning a Caddy. Rocco was no exception.

Blackie felt secure with his plan, and tonight was the night. He wore all black to blend in with the nocturnal blanket, and the garrote was securely in his hands, ready to do its duty. He found a small alcove along the bushes where he could hide safely and be able to jump out and surprise LaPearl from behind. Blackie was ready to finish the job once and for all. He cared little about the reason that LaPearl had to be taken out; his main concern was the money, and the money was first and foremost.

Rocco listened to the sounds of the night as he strode along High Street toward his destination on Walnut Avenue. He seemed to have an extra bounce in his step when he came from one of Garrett's games. Tonight was no exception. The rodent-like sinister eyes of Blackie Beans were upon him immediately when Rocky left the gym. Colombo had picked an ideal location from an observatory standpoint to monitor LaPearl's movements. As he came closer and closer to the deadly trap, Rocky felt as though he was being watched, as if he had a third eye or something, and became extremely wary of his surroundings. Closer and closer to his deathtrap he came, his nocturnal antennae at the peak of its power. With about five paces to go, Rocco LaPearl, with split-second timing, decided to cross the street just three yards short of the deadly hiding place. The plan had been spoiled. LaPearl was out of harm's way, and Blackie was irate.

"That mothafucker is one lucky dude. I'll get him yet. He's a dead man. It's just a matter of time."

Both men left the area for different reasons and went about their ways. Call it a stroke of luck or simply the ways of the streets, for now Rocco was safe.

# ENGLAND

Nasta was beginning to feel more comfortable in England now. After six long tedious months, she was becoming a Brit through the process of force-feeding the British ways. *The Brightons were doing a marvelous job*, she thought. *They were very diligent about what they were teaching, so why not go with the flow?*

Anastasia was sitting in class, no other students, just her, as usual, daydreaming and longing to go home for vacation. It was a beautiful spring day in England. As Ms. Pruitt, the economics teacher, was chattering about something of national importance, Nasta felt something smack her in the back of the head. It was Heir Gunther who just happened to be walking down the hall of the academics building and spotted Anastasia falling asleep in class. He quietly opened the classroom door, snuck in, and checked Nasta.

"What the frig is wrong with you?" Heir Gunther was her pet name for the athletic German. "Are you crazy?"

"That will be fifty push-ups now!" screamed Gunther. "Nowwwwwww!"

Nasta did the fifty easily and slithered back into the chair.

"Please forgive me, Ms. Pruitt, but I caught her not paying attention." Nasta chuckled to herself at the rhetoric between the two instructors. She laughed because one night when she couldn't sleep and she got out of bed to get a glass of milk, she heard a moaning noise in a seldom-used utility room on the third floor of her dorm. She went up to that floor and saw Heir Gunther and Ms. Pruitt putting their clothes back on, obviously the end of a passionate lovemaking session. They both looked exhausted and very, very satisfied.

"What is so funny?" Ms. Pruitt asked Nasta.

"Oh, nothing, Ms. P."

"Let's continue then, young lady, time is our enemy."

*Now why would she use a word like* enemy? thought Nasta with a quizzical look on her face.

"It is important for you to learn the economic status of all the large prosperous countries in the world. We will learn other currencies, their formal government, and who their leaders are, both good and evil. You will know the names of every president in every country in the entire world."

"Why?" asked Nasta.

"Because the Brightons and I say so, that's why. Now let us continue, please."

The economics class lasted three hours and was attended by Nasta three days per week. The young girl hated that class and Ms. P., but she had to admit it was quite interesting.

After economics, Nasta had an hour of free time. She was basically permitted to relax, wander the campus, and basically do anything she wanted. What she did not know was that there were surveillance cameras hidden from view everywhere. The Brightons kept a watchful eye on their pupil and monitored her every movement.

Nasta was walking along the tree-lined path, heading toward the gymnasium. *What a nice day*, thought the sixteen–year–old Slavic beauty. *I could just climb that big old fence and run like the wind straight for the train station.* As she pondered this thought, she noticed a large shed or storage garage just at the north end of the gym. *I have never noticed that before. Umm, probably another place for Gunther and Ms. P. get the yah yahs.* She laughed aloud and continued along the path toward this shed. While approaching, she noticed a keylock dangling from the door to the garage, and it appeared to be unlocked, the key still inserted in the lock. *My good luck*, she thought. *Let's see what this is all about.*

She pulled open the door all the way and peered inside. She first noticed shelves from the floor almost up to the ceiling, very clean and organized. Nothing out of the ordinary. Most of the crates and boxes were unopened, and the labels read "Steel products do not open." The boxes appeared to be about eight to ten feet long, grayish in color. Hundreds, perhaps even a thousand of them.

"What the hell are these things? It says do not touch, but who cares. The worst that could happen is that I get sent home." Nasta slowly approached one of the crates and looked it over carefully. "These boxes look like they came from the military. I'll bet Nigel is some type of arms dealer." She laughed. Nasta looked around the dimly lit room for a crowbar or something that could pry open the crate. Finally, she found a long piece of metal, a hinge of some sort, and began the task of prying open the crate. Beads of sweat were forming on her forehead. Even though everything here was a joke to her, she was still quite nervous.

Working feverishly on the box, fearing the worst, getting caught, Nasta was finally able to get it open. There, glistening in the half-lit room, were rows and rows of metal plates, the kind used for all types of construction projects, very unusual to be stored in a school. As Nasta was about to walk away, she noticed some plastic wrapping sticking out of one of the rows of steel. She carefully lifted three of the pieces of metal and noticed several smaller boxes neatly lined up side by side. She thought the boxes were shaped square, for the most part, and yet they also had a long cylindrical shape at the bottom. Her curiosity level was way up, so she figured why not. The worst that could happen was they would send her home. She ripped off the outer layer of plastic and flipped open the lid.

"Holy shit, guns!" she screamed loud enough to startle herself. Guns in all shapes and sizes. The longer cylinder-like areas of the boxes contained attachments similar to what she once saw in a James Bond movie that muffled the sound of the gunshot. It kept the sound silenced. "Silencers, that's what they were called. Yeah, that's it. What the frig are these doing in a school? I'd better get the frig out of here now! The Brightons have some explaining to do. I'd better be extra careful."

Nasta put everything back the way she found it and carefully slipped out the way she came in. *This place is starting to give me the creeps.* She ran as fast as she could back toward the dorm, not noticing a long black limo approaching the main gates of the complex heading right in Nasta's direction. Nasta was running like a cheetah, but she kept looking back to see if anyone was following her. All of a sudden, with catlike reflexes, she instinctively turned her head to the front, saw the limo, and dodged it as if by some stroke of magic. She avoided getting hit by about three inches. She would have been hurt quite badly. Not even bothering to slow down, she continued her sprint toward the dorm and flew up the staircase and into the shelter of her bedroom.

The limo eased its way into a parking area as if nothing happened. The limo driver swung open his door and got out. Dressed in the typical mobile servants garb, black jacket and pants, white shirt, and of course, sitting on top of his head was the usual chapeau, very British indeed. The passengers waited until their doors were opened for them and got out onto the sidewalk. Both men were quite tall and well dressed. The finest wool-blend suits with silk ties, Kenneth Cole shoes, and one of the men seemed to walk with a limp on his right leg and he carried a fine oak walking stick with the head of a cobra made of 24K gold. Nigel Brighton arrived just at that moment and ushered the two men into the main building.

"Please sit down in the study, and please make yourself at home. The bar is well stocked, especially with the finest twelve-year-old scotch. I'll be back in a moment. Gentlemen, I must do another check to see if anyone is trying to listen in on us." Both men took their seats as directed and waited for Nigel to return. "No one's in sight, so let's proceed, gentlemen."

Nigel took his place in the center of the room, both men following his every movement as if rehearsed. Nigel pressed a red button on a hidden panel and a screen lowered down from the ceiling. A projector buzzed, showing a picture of young Nasta, dressed in very short shorts, a Guinea T-shirt, standing in her bare feet. "Here she is, gentlemen, Anastasia Bohinj. Our pride and joy," said Nigel. "What do you think?"

"She's perfect!" yelled the one stranger. "Just perfect from what I see. I can tell you have worked on her body strength. She is quite muscular, very long and lean. But can she do what we ask her to do? Does she have the stomach for this kind of work?"

"We feel she does, Sir George. She is multitalented with many facets. Allow me to proceed with the film."

The first scene showed Nasta in a small roped-off area with boxing gloves on. Suddenly, out of nowhere, a man came into the picture from behind Anastasia. With catlike reflexes, Nasta whirled around just in the nick of time and landed a punch square on the jaw of the would-be attacker. He went down like a ton of bricks. Nasta stood over her victim with a cold smile on her face and, not knowing she was being filmed, raised her fists in the air in triumph. Both Sir George and the other man nodded in approval at the young girl's victory.

"Wow, is she quick, or is she quick, gentlemen? She seems to enjoy this type of thing, don't you agree, my friends? Let's continue."

For the next hour, the three men watched Nasta in her comings and goings during her daily routines. They observed her in class as the only student, and they were able to see her interact with Sir Nigel's kids as well. She always seemed to demand all the attention in her actions with others. She seemed to thrive on having the upper hand. Both men were equally impressed with the young girl as they stood and prepared to leave.

"She is absolutely perfect," said Sir George. "I am very impressed with your choice, Nigel."

"Indeed," said the other. "Excellent choice indeed."

"Thank you, gentlemen. I'm glad you feel the same way. Six more months and we will have the finished product."

As both men entered the limo, Nigel Brighton stood in the doorway with a wide grin on his face for several moments. Little did he know that Nasta lowered a string tied to a mirror so she could watch Nigel as the men departed. *With a shit-eaten grin,* thought Nasta. She had acquired the American phrase from some movie magazine she had smuggled into the dorm when she arrived. *What the hell is he smiling at, and who the frig were those men?*

# Garrett in Haddon Hills, New Jersey

Garrett was already at home, showered and relaxed after the game. He was waiting for his father to get home so they could talk basketball. Even though Rocco had never played the game himself, by watching his son, he had learned quite a bit. Garrett heard the backdoor open and wondered why his father came in that entrance as he usually came in through the front.

"Hey, Pops, I am in the living room, come on in."

"Okay, son, I'll be right there." Rocco entered the neat and tidy living room and immediately settled into his favorite recliner made of the finest leather. He stretched out into full recline and was ready to chat.

"How come you came through the back, Dad?"

"Oh, just to keep things from getting boring."

Knowing something about his father's secret life, Garrett didn't totally believe him. "So how did I play tonight? Was I any good?"

"Well—you were *menza menz.*"

"What?" shrieked Garrett.

"Just kidding, little man. You were awesome, simply awesome."

"Coming from you that is high praise, Pops." Garrett was referring to his father's low-key personality. Not one to dole out compliments too readily. "You played the conservative all-around game, and I am very proud and pleased with you. One thing about you, my boy, you can handle all aspects of the game."

"Thanks, Pops, it's called mastering the game. Something I always aspired to do right from the beginning. Father Jack always preached that to me. I can still hear him shouting 'master the game,' repeating it over and over."

Rocco sat back in his recliner and watched his son watching the television. He seemed to be growing right before his eyes. *I hope that I live long enough to see you become a man,* thought Rocco. *In my crazy world anything is likely to happen.*

At that very moment, a hail of bullets ripped through the large front room windows. Glass and pieces of furniture were scattered everywhere. The first gun burst met its mark; unfortunately, two bullets to the heart and Rocco was dead. It was a lie.

Dead in his own home, endangering his family, not the typical mob hit. Garrett burst into the living room, tears pouring down his face, looking and hoping his father was still alive. Fragments of glass and wood crackled under his feet as he continued to search the room. He heard a sound directly behind him, and he whirled around, crouching like a tiger ready to pounce on his prey just like his father had taught him. Standing there with a devastated look on his face, completely ashen in color, was his mother. Garrett quickly ran to her and held her in his arms. She was shaking like a leaf as light as a feather. For an instant, Garrett thought of lifting her up and carrying her away form this insanity. She began to scream as she looked to her right. There, behind the sofa, lay her lover's bullet-torn body.

"Noooooooooooo!" she screamed; the sound of her voice echoed throughout the room. The sound was deafening as she continued to scream. "Why, why, why!" she shouted. "Why would they kill my Rocco?" Garrett acted quickly, locating a blanket and covering his father's body. "In our home, in our home!" Fiona screamed. "Jesus Christ in heaven."

Garrett, although stunned and more than likely in shock, quickly embraced his mother and slowly led her out of the bloody scene. His thoughts were varied, and racing quickly through his head was the idea of getting away from the house. Maybe the assholes were paid to finish everyone in the family or maybe not. He couldn't take that chance. It was only him and Fiona. Joseph was away at college in northern New Jersey. All three cars, his Mustang, the Cadillac, and the SUV were parked next to the house, adjacent to the garage. The villain or villains could be lying in wait in the many hiding places in their expansive yard. Garrett thought that he would act as a decoy to draw their fire. So he stepped out on the patio. Ten seconds, twenty seconds, one minute. Nothing. The chance to make their move is now. He quickly ran back into the house to get his mother in the library where he had left her and instructed her not to move. Fiona was nowhere to be found. "Where the fuck?" The silence in the house was deafening. He thought he heard a faint sound coming from the living room, where his father's bullet-torn body was lying there next to the fireplace, wrapped in a five-thousand-dollar Persian rug. Fiona had slipped back into the room to say good-bye once more to her lifelong sweetheart. She was sobbing uncontrollably when Garrett reached her and began to coax her out of the room.

"Come, Mother, we must get out of here. Please let's go." They sped quickly and silently out of the crime scene onto the patio and jumped into the silver-colored vehicle. Garrett started the ignition and slammed it into reverse. The car accelerated down the driveway in a flash. Just as they were about to leave the driveway, the police arrived. Flashing lights and uniforms everywhere. Garrett and Fiona sat back and waited for the police to take over. Blackie Beans had accomplished his mission. The hit went smoothly and efficiently. He had decided about two weeks ago to abandon the garrote and use an Uzi automatic weapon to be sure to take LaPearl out. A bit noisy but it gets the job done. He would have to explain to his superiors why he made the hit in the guy's home. But it would be no problem because the problem was dead. Simple as that to a hired killer. *That motherf——r won't create any more problems*, thought Blackie. *I heard he wasn't a bad guy at all, but a threat to take over nonetheless.*

*The life of a wiseguy, the crazy life of a wiseguy . . . friggen crazy.*

Three days later, Garrett woke up from a sound sleep, sweating profusely. Since the tragedy of his father's death occurred, he hadn't slept well at all. He was constantly worried about his mother and, who knows, maybe even his brother. Garrett had developed survival instincts from his father over the years that were starting to surface. "Protect your loved ones at all cost. Cover your bases, cover your bases," his father would preach to him. "Make sure all the angles are taken care of if something happens to me."

Rocco had told his son about a substantial amount of money in a safety deposit box in a bank in upstate New Jersey. The town of Old Bridge was about seventy-five miles away. Garrett knew that he would need this money to tie up loose ends and other things as well. His distraught mother was his main priority right at the moment. Her depression was so deep it appeared as though nothing could help her. Garrett acted quickly and hired the best counselor in the area, one Betty Simberg. At three hundred dollars per hour, she had better be good. Fiona was slipping away into a state of total denial that her husband was dead and needed constant attention to help her through this horrible, horrible tragedy.

Garrett, wise beyond his years, knew he could only do so much. Hopeful that given time, his mother, only forty-seven years old, would recover and put her life back together. She was very attractive and would easily find another companion if she chose to do so.

# ENGLAND

It was Saturday, and Nasta assumed that she would be given the day off. If for anything, as a reward for being so good at everything. Old Nigel seemed to be very pleased with her of late. Of course, he never welcomes her rebellious antics and sneers, at her lack of table manners and good old-fashioned etiquette. Nasta thinks nothing of letting out a large guttural belch at the dinner table and laughs until she cries to see the look of disgust on Nigel and Margaret's face. But watching their young pupil develop into one of the best in the world at what she does far outweighs her antics.

"What do you mean I can't leave the place for a couple of hours?" yelled Nasta. "It's friggen Saturday. I want to go out. You've kept me on a leash long enough."

"No. N-o!" yelled Nigel. "Tone your voice down and

come with me. I have something to show you that we think you will really like."

"What now, Nigel?" complained Nasta.

"Come, you'll see."

Nigel led Nasta over to the far left corner of the property. An area that contained a long building with a low roof, it almost resembled a chicken coup. Oddly, it had no windows on it. Nasta had never been over to this part of the property and wondered why old Brighton was taking her there. When they arrived at the front door, Nigel pulled out a large keychain with about four or five keys on it. Nasta, always the thinker, tried to remember which key it was.

"Why, Nigel, old boy, this place looks like a building with no purpose," Nigel replied. "It has a very very important purpose, indeed."

"Indeed!" shouted Nasta. "What's new?"

As the two entered the long room, the smell of something caught Nasta's nasal attention. "What is that smell, Nigel?"

Back in Slovenia, growing up in Cerknica, many people owned a gun for hunting or just plain old protection. The smell that she had referred to was gunpowder. "That's it, after someone shoots a gun, that smell is left drifting in the air."

"You are absolutely correct," said Nigel. "This is the shooting range where you will learn about every gun in existence. Well, almost every gun. We believe knowledge of guns is very important to anyone in their daily existence. Part of your schooling requires you to become an expert in weaponry, both the practical usage and of course the inner workings. The assembly of each different gun and how best to get the maximum efficiency from each and every type of gun. Handguns, rifles, rocket launchers concealed in everyday luggage. Guns will be brought to your attention. Quite simply, you will become nothing less than an expert of weaponry."

"If you say so, Mr. Nigel, sir." There was a hint of sarcasm in Nasta's voice as usual, and Nigel picked up on it right away.

"Now, young lady, you will learn to obey, and if I have to employ other methods to get you to comply, I will."

"Sure, Nigel, is that a threat? Tell me more about these so-called methods."

Nigel's face turned bright red, and his eyes started to bulge right out of the sockets. "Okay, have it your way, Ms. Stubborn!" shouted Nigel.

With that, Nigel whistled the loudest Nasta had ever heard someone whistle. The sound of running feet could be heard in the distance. Nigel's assistant, Igor, came charging into the room. "Take her to the room, and put her in the stocks." Igor grabbed Nasta by the hair and literally dragged her down the long hallway to the room. "Have some fun with her if you want."

*What did he mean by that?* thought Nasta. *And what the f—— is the room.* "Ouch, not so hard, Gor, take it easy."

As they entered the room, Nasta saw what looked to be a piece of furniture of sorts, very old, but very sturdy-looking.

"What is that?"

"The stocks," said Igor. "Keep quiet and do not resist." With that, Igor forced Nasta to sit down in the middle of the contraption and immediately felt her arms being pulled back and up above her head. She could feel her wrists being placed in some kind of restraint, shackles of some sort. After completing that, Nasta's feet were forced through two round holes with a board attached so she couldn't see her feet.

"Get me out of this thing, you weirdo."

"No way, not until I torture you for a while."

*Torture*, thought Nasta. *Are these people nuts?* Securely in place, Nasta began to squirm a bit, sensing something uncomfortable was about to occur. Igor went to the end where Nasta's feet were and knelt down. He began untying Nasta's shoes and removing them. He began to tickle the bottoms of Nasta's feet. He had very long fingernails, which she could feel right through her socks. "No, stop, I am very ticklish on my feet. Stop."

Igor didn't seem to be paying attention and kept right on tickling. Nasta couldn't stop laughing. About ten minutes went by before Igor pulled her socks off he began to really tickle her now. Nasta was going nuts. "Stoppppp, you just wait until I get out of this thing."

"Just relax and enjoy." A few minutes later, Igor stopped and walked over to a workbench, picked up a bottle of oil, and proceeded to rub it over the bottom of Nasta's feet. The sensation she now felt was ten times worse, and her laughter got louder and louder. Igor had a big smile on his face. "I'll do anything, please stop tickling my feet."

"No way, only if you promise never to disobey Nigel again. Back in the 1600s, these methods were used on adulterers, and it worked very well," said Igor. "Why not now?"

He next picked some string lying on the floor. Nasta had noticed it earlier but couldn't figure out what Igor had in mind for it. He then looped the string of her left foot and put the string through an eyehole and pulled it tight so the bottom of Nasta's feet were protruding forward. He did the same with the other foot also. He now began to apply the oil on her foot bottoms some more and started to tickle again. Nasta felt the tickling sensation even more now. "Stop. Stop. Stop. I can't take it much longer," she cried.

"Well then, so shall we call it a day?" shouted Igor. "But I am having too much fun. I do not want to stop."

Just then, the door flew open and in walked Nigel. "Enough. Now, Igor, untie her and go about your business. The guns in the weapon room need cleaning. Get to it."

With that, Igor sauntered out with a devilish grin on this face.

"Well now, young lady, have you had enough?"

"Yes, Nigel. Please get me out of here. I will do as I am told without questions and no more wisecracks." Nigel untied Nasta and helper her out of the torture contraption.

She gave him a sinister look as if to say "I will get revenge on you and the rest of those strange people someday, maybe sooner than later." Nigel caught the glare out of the corner of his eye, just as a trained operative would use his or her peripheral vision, and smiled. He sure would like the cavalier attitude that she exhibited as he knew she would need it later on in her newfound career.

"Were you glad to be out of that predicament? That guy was enjoying it too much. Nasta, understand that Igor is merely a drone here. He merely does what he's told and no more. We don't even want him to think, only to obey."

"I see," said Nasta. "I believe I know the hierarchy of authority here. It's becoming clearer and clearer."

"Why don't you go up to your room, get cleaned up, and ready yourself for dinner. We have a special guest coming in, and I would like you to be ready for him. He is a British citizen, but was born in Germany. His name is Thomas Mark."

Heir Mark was born in Stuttgart, but lived in Berlin most of his life. At fifty-eight years old, he is beginning to show signs of aging, but with vast fortune, he enjoyed the finest medicine and alternatives to keep him looking healthy and fit. His mother was a baroness with real estate holdings all over the world. She died five years ago at the age of eighty-six. His father was a general in the German army and a staunch supporter of the Nazi regime in World War II. His father disappeared right after the war, never to be heard from again. It is believed that he fled to South America and lived to be ninety-three years old. His vast fortune had yet to be claimed. Thomas was cut from his father's cloth, inheriting the same gall that helped his father flourish during and after the war. Thomas is cunning and clever and knows how to blend in when necessary. Sir Nigel became suspicious of Heir Mark five years ago concerning some drug-related activities in the heroin region of Cambodia. Sources revealed that Heir Mark not only worked for the British government but also dabbled in the international drug market that stretched from the Far East to the major cities of North America and beyond. Thomas was not aware of Nigel's suspicions.

Nasta was just finished getting dressed when she heard the brass door knocker made contact with the oak front door. Igor ushered Heir Mark into the stateroom just as Nasta was gliding down the magnificent stairway. Sometimes she would sit on the railing and slide all the way down. Heir Mark was dressed in a gray single-breasted tweed suit, probably from Savile Row. *It looks very expensive,* she thought. She also noticed that his shoes were impeccably polished. "A rather dapper fellow," sputtered Nasta. Before Nasta stepped down off the last step, Sir Nigel appeared to greet Heir Mark.

"Hello, Tom," said Nigel. "How's it going?"

"Very good. Young lady, who may you be?"

"I am Anastasia Bohinj, and I am a student here at the school."

"Very good," said Thomas. "And my name is Thomas."

"Okay," said Nasta. "Thomas it is."

They entered the dining room and proceeded to take their place at the large cherrywood dining room table. The place settings had been set two hours earlier by the chambermaids who then were given the remainder of the day off. Nigel did not want any outside interference to affect their very important meeting. As usual, Nigel sat at the head of the table, Heir Mark to his right, and Nasta to his left.

"Well now, this is really nice having dinner with both of you," said Nigel. "I hope you enjoy the succulent lamb roast prepared by in-house staff. It is quite wonderful."

Nasta was paying attention, but she couldn't take her eyes off Heir Mark. At the moment, she didn't know if she liked this man or not. There was something odd about him.

"I haven't had lamb in ages, Nigel. This will be a treat, I'm sure. Please pass the red wine if you don't mind, and, Nigel, bon appetite."

Not looking Nasta's way for he did realize that she was too young to drink alcohol. After he had spread mint jelly over his entrée, Heir Mark began to eat like he hadn't had food in a week. *It is funny how such a rich and successful well ??? man could eat like a goddamned glutton*, thought Nasta. *Too funny. This guy belongs in a zoo.* Nasta thought of this while she had a smile on her face, looking Heir Mark right in the eyes. Right into those pale green sinister evil eyes. *Whew,* sighed Nasta. *I would not want to meet him alone in a dark alley.*

Young Nasta was becoming quite adept at acting one way and thinking about the opposite. Her side to side vision had become excellent through her yoga eye training. She was training with Lady Catherine, her instructor. Yoga would play a big part in her developing a strong agile body. As she studied Thomas Mark out of the corner of her eye, she noticed he never once looked her way with any type of appeal or wonderment. *Oh well,* she thought. *Screw him.*

After finally laying his torte to rest, Thomas Mark finally began to relax. "Cognac, Heir Mark?" said Nigel.

"Don't mind if I do, and how about one of those fine Dominican cigars. I prefer Cuban, but these will do."

"Did you know that Castro favors the Dominican cigar to the Cuban?" Nigel claimed.

"No, I did not," retorted Thomas with a slight hint of sarcasm in his voice. "Who cares anyway? Now let's get down to business. I have a problem, and you claim that you can make it go away. My people in Cambodia are dropping like flies over there at the hands of Pol Chen, a very powerful overlord and despot. If he is taken out, I am free to harvest as much of the poppy fields as I want, and the heroin trade will flourish once again."

"Nasta, don't you have some homework to do?" Nigel calmly said. "Please go and tend to your responsibilities."

Nasta, with a puzzled look on her face, got up from the large table and shuffled away. *Just when it was getting good, he tells me to leave.* Nigel had set the stage earlier, allowing Nasta to hear a little of the reason why Mark was there and then ask her to leave. *What a prick*, thought Nasta. *I was just getting into it.*

Nigel was brilliant at training young operatives. Give them a bone then take it away. Just like a well-trained killer dog. Only this dog walked upright and would one day be the very best in the world.

"Pol Chen is controlling that region with an iron fist, Nigel. He's gotta be taken out. Nowwwwww. Do you understand me? Nowwww. I am losing five to six million pounds a day. I can't absorb that amount much longer. His men are raping the women that live there, and his hit squads are not only raping but they are methodically killing the men. Nigel, let's move on it now. Who do you have in your stable of killers to pull this one off? I am the only one Chen trusts to be near him."

# NINE YEARS LATER
# GARRETT NASTA

Twenty-one-year-old Garrett "Gary" LaPearl stepped off the plane to be greeted by the deliciously warm Italian sun. It was a beautiful day in Rome, and Garrett welcomed the change from the USA. It was the worst spring in recent memory, and all the traveling Americans seemed very uptight. He and Fiona had decided to come to the country of their origin and enjoy the wonderful sights of Rome. It had been nine long years since his father's death, and so he wanted to put the past completely behind him. Even after all these years, young Garrett still felt the great loss of his father. Sometimes his chest would swell as he thought about acts of revenge. It made him feel proud, proud to be an Italian American with underworld ties.

La Familia—the old wiseguys would say the family is

the main entity in their lives. Their children were always first, and their wives and mistresses came second. Italian mobsters, no matter where they hailed from, had a mistress stashed somewhere. Rocco LaPearl had alluded to his son Garrett many years ago that he was no different, but his wife Fiona was the focal point of his life. Garrett, always the do-gooder, was glad, for he knew the ways of the mob simply because he grew up under that way of thinking.

"Revenge was a dish enjoyed most when it was cold," his father would say. "Do not react, my son. Respond to the situation. Be prepared when you seek revenge or else it will turn its ugly head to you. You will become the victim."

Garrett was smart and capable at twenty-one, but living for revenge was not really his way. He did not want to be a made guy, to do a piece of work for the mob or anybody, like his father and uncles did. No, he would become a lawyer or an accountant on his own business. Something legit. He laughed. "Yeah, sure."

Nine years ago, his father had left a parting letter about some money he had accumulated for a rainy day in Old Bridge, New Jersey. Somewhere young Garrett had yet to go, and he never told his mother. Fiona was well taken care of by her husband, Garrett, and Joseph. They inherited money, some houses, particularly a house at the Jersey shore under the name of Rocco's mother. Now it belonged to Garrett, an estimated worth of about six hundred fifty thousand dollars.

# WHEN IN ROME

Fiona and Garrett checked into a room in arguably the finest hotel in all of Italy. The Etruscan was located within some of the most famous attractions in the Eternal City. Within walking distance were the Colosseum, Trevi Fountain, the seven hills, and many more. The Etruscan was said to be booked at least two years in advance. Garrett gave them one month notice, and with family connections, the plan was for Garrett and Fiona to spend one week together in Rome then go their separate ways. Fiona's first cousin Angelica lived close to the hotel, so they were to rendezvous on Wednesday to see the Pope. Garrett had acquired a Eurail pass (unlimited train travel) and was anxiously awaiting his adventure. Ever since he was five years old, he talked of traveling. Where this mysterious notion came from, nobody knew.

As they entered the hotel, both were amazed at the beauty and splendor of the hotel. Built in the 1500s and later renovated in 1948 after the war, it was truly magnificent. The color gold was everywhere, from the top of the lavish archways to the marble floor—truly magnificent. Garrett imagined the nightly fee to be around one thousand American dollars per night or about five thousand lira. They were greeted in the great vestibule by six young men dressed in outfits, each one impeccable. They all had specific responsibilities centered on pleasing their newest arrivals. After check-in, they were ushered to the very top room of the hotel. The panoramic view was truly remarkable as Fiona threw open the balcony doors. The city of Rome was literally out her backdoor. Fiona felt the warm sensation throughout her body as it finally hit her that she was standing on the balcony of the most visited city in the entire world. As sad as she was, she felt herself just now beginning to relax. "Ahhhh," she sighed. "What a view. Pinch me, Garrett, pinch me so that I know that I am here."

Garrett moved closer to his mother and wrapped his arms around her. "Yes, Mother, we are really here, and we are going to have a great time."

"Let's start by getting something to eat. You know, when in Rome, do as the Romans do. Do we order room service, or would you care to be my date for the evening?"

"Your date of course," uttered Garrett. "I know you will be the prettiest woman in any restaurant. I will ask the people at the front desk their opinion as to which is the best eatery close to the hotel." Fiona nodded in approval. "Perhaps we could eat right here in the hotel. I think I would enjoy that."

With jet lag starting to set in, Fiona was growing more and more tired after the long flight. Garrett stepped into the plush elevator, encountering four other people in the spacious indoor taxi. One of the patrons was quite odd, remarkably different than the others, as if he didn't belong. He stood about six feet five inches. Garrett accurately guessed the man's height from his basketball experience. His hair was long with golden-colored ringlets throughout his head, hanging down on his shoulders. He was dressed like he had just gotten off the Banana Republic photo shoot—very stylish and yet very unique from the other hotel guests. He seemed to be beckoning for his attention. Garrett noticed the man's eyes when without hesitation he looked at Garrett right in the eye and smiled. His eyes were green, the color of a Bahamian inlet. They were piercing and beguiling at the same time. *He had the kind of stare that could totally relax you or totally scare the hell out of you*, thought Garrett. Without a doubt this man stood out. The whole ride in the elevator, this modern-day dashing pirate was flipping a gold dollar piece. Up and down, up and down, the sound of his well-manicured fingernails flipping the coin. If you stared at it long enough, it would more than likely have a hypnotic effect.

Jack D'Amberville was a man's man and a little bit more. The whispers on the street were that D'Amberville bedded more than two thousand women from all over the world. He possessed that rare charm that women adored. Yes, Jackson D'Amberville was quite a ladies' man. They say the best coaches in sports are former players, a players coach. Well D'Amberville was just that, the ladies' man.

# LONDON

It was a rare day indeed when Anastasia could get away from the compound as she referred to it. The sun boldly broadcasted its arrival with astounding radiance. It felt so good on her clear face, she thought as she strode along the city streets. The vendors and store owners were out in force, ready to turn a pound or two. One particular rather peculiar vendor, a woman, caught Nasta's eye. As she felt herself staring, the old woman turned her wrinkled face in Nasta's direction.

Immediately, they made eye contact. "Come, my lovely young thing, come and behold the most beautiful rose in the world." An incorrigible skeptic, Nasta right away backed away. "Don't be shy, young lady. I won't bite you."

She was dressed in an old frumpy-looking dress, a bit tattered, but clean just the same. Her hair was swept up in a tight bun. Upon closer examination, she was quite lovely. Nasta thought her voice was a shrill cockney sound. Of course, we are in London.

"This is the most unusual rose in the universe, lovely lady, and you will have the chance to own it. A black rose. Nowhere on earth can you get the black rose, only from me. I was chosen to own and sell the specimen." Nasta bent down as the old lady opened a separate box full of those unusual flowers. "Black, black as coal," she wailed. "Especially for you because you were chosen by the black rose." Nasta could not believe the hypnotic effect this old lady had on her. She felt sort of dizzy like in a trance, on the verge of passing out.

"Wow, I don't feel well. Ah, ah, I didn't get your name," said Nasta.

"I didn't give it," the old woman shot back. "What is a name anyway?"

Nasta hesitantly blurted out, "We need it to be identified, that's all." With that, she said, "Why am I even talking to this weird character?"

"Why? Take one home with you. Here, girl, take one home. Put it in a pretty vase, and gaze upon its elegance. It will alter your moods every day in a different manner, you'll see. Here, take this one, freshly cut and groomed just for you, for I knew you were coming."

Nasta took the flower reluctantly. As she reached out to grab the rose, she immediately felt the prick on her index finger. Blood appeared right away. The old woman apologetically wrapped it and offered a Band-Aid. Nasta refused. "I'll get one at home." She just wanted to get away from there. *How weird was that?* she thought.

There was soft knock on Nigel's door of his study. "Come in, please and sit down. How did it go, Mary?"

"She fell for it hook, line, and sinker or whatever that Yankee saying is."

"Dear girl, you must keep up on these things." They both laughed.

Mary Tunsfill was forty years old, but with the right makeup, she looked eighty. Mary was busy peeling off the fake skin as Nigel sat there looking on. "Young Nasta had no idea that I was anyone but a vendor of black-colored roses. She was receptive and cooperative after I did some good old British thespianism."

"Well done, Mary, very well indeed," said Nigel. "I do

believe we have accomplished a good part of our project, don't you, old girl?"

Mary nodded with approval. "She's primed and ready now, Sir Nigel. The black rose will begin the odyssey."

Nasta got back to the compound and ran quickly up the staircase in the great hall and looked immediately for a vase or a bottle or something. She made darn sure there were no thorns on it this time. *I'm going to try and keep it at bay as long as possible.* Exhausted from a long day of walking the streets of London, away from everyone, she kicked off her shoes and fell fast asleep. Her first dream was about the old lady and her flowers and about her very own prize.

Nasta was a young lady of a myriad of personality traits. It was almost odd that she had a soft side as well. She seemed to swing from one mood to another, the violent side being one of them.

Garrett got off the elevator and broke away from the others and headed for the streets. He almost seemed to be running, showing his anxiousness. "Finally, I am in Rome, the most visited city in the world. Roma as the natives say. The Eternal City." Garrett stopped suddenly and looked around. He had the feeling someone was watching him, as if he possessed a third eye or radar. Looking up and down the cobblestone Via Venezia, he thought, *I am paranoid. I don't see anything except throngs of people milling about.* He had quickly flashed back to that fateful night when his father was assassinated. He truly was paranoid and rightfully so; his father, you recall, was gunned down in his own home. *Perhaps they are here hunting me as well.*

"Stay cool," his father used to say. "Stay calm and you will see more. You'll eventually be able to read between the lines, an asset all of us would like to possess."

Garrett continued along the Via Venezia, taking in the sights. He observed that many cars in Rome were undamaged, without dents and scratches, not like the United States where so many cars had blemishes on them. *People here seemed to be in a hurry just like back home*, he thought, but they were more careful, moving at a slower pace. Garrett noticed a young woman walking on the other side of the street. He guessed her age to be around the same as his, twenty-one or twenty-two, something like that. She was walking very slowly, simply taking in the sights, window shopping, and of course, women are always buying something. He thought, *New clothes, shoes, or jewelry. Boy would I like to meet her.*

When it came to the opposite sex, Garrett was a bit shy, almost nonaggressive. Although at home he had a few girls in his sweet short life, why would this be any different? As he continued his walk, he marveled at some of the antiques that he saw.

*I want to go to the Colosseum*, he thought. *I must see that among many other sites.* His adrenaline was starting to rise. *Here I am in Roma. It is April, and the weather is starting to break. Oh yeah, my mother and I are going to put our worries aside and have a blast. She really needs this vacation after losing her husband of thirty-three years. I miss him dearly.*

Garrett was talking to himself as he sauntered along when he began to get very hungry. *Where can I stop for a bite to eat? I wonder if they have pizza here like at home,* he thought. *It's probably not half as good as ours. We have the best of everything. I'll just look around and find a place with the word "restaurant" on the front windows and go in.*

Garrett walked another three blocks when he noticed a place that had outdoor seating and many patrons sitting at small tables, talking and laughing as they were sipping a glass of wine, enjoying life. He sat down at an empty one and waited for someone to take his order.

"Buongiorno, señor," said a young man with a notepad. "May I take your order?"

Garrett was amazed that the guy spoke good English. "Why, you speak English very well. How did you know I was American?"

"Believe me, señor, it's quite obvious. I can spot an American a mile away." They both laughed.

"Give me a small pizza and a glass of red wine."

"Grazie, señor. It will be out shortly."

Garrett was enjoying his surroundings when all of a sudden, the girl he had seen before was walking straight toward the café, right toward him. "Boy I hope she sits at the next table right next to mine. That would be awesome." Sure enough the young woman sat right next to Garrett. Suddenly, he felt a burning sensation in his loins. She was even more beautiful up close. Garrett felt himself staring and quickly looked away so he would not make eye contact. He was playing it cool. She was dressed in a peach-colored skirt with a black tie. Her legs were bare and on her feet were two-inch heels. *Probably very expensive*, he thought.

He was watching as she sat down and immediately slid her feet out of her shoes. Her legs were eye-catching and well taken care of. She glanced over at Garrett who sat only a few feet away, smiled, and said, "My feet are killing me in these shoes." Her accent was definitely Italian. Garrett smiled back at her when just at that moment, his food arrived, and her waiter approached to take her order.

Ashlina Graffo was a sight to behold. Ocean blue eyes and a turned up nose. About five feet two inches tall, Ashlina was a natural beauty. She liked to wear her hair swept up to a tight well-kept heap upon her head. When released, her blond mane cascaded down, well past her shoulders. She had a trim, well-kept body that was actually covered by only the finest designer in the world. Ash, as she is called by the people in Sicily, liked to wear three-inch stiletto heels everywhere. She would look for some unsuspecting man at the end of the day to run her aching feet. Ashlina was as flirtatious as they come. Her father, Francesco Graffo, it was said, was a millionaire many times over. Some said his fortune was estimated at close to one billion. He owned oil companies, vast real estate holdings, and even his own island somewhere in the Aegean Sea. Ashlina would inherit it all someday.

Garrett was crunching on his pizza when suddenly he

heard her say something aloud, seemingly directed toward him. "Scusa, señor, do you speak English?"

Garrett paused for a moment. "Sure, yes, of course," he stammered. "I do."

"Belle," she said in broken English, "how are you today?"

"And you," said Garrett, "how are you?"

"Wonderful I am except for my feet. They hurt from these shoes so much."

"Well, I would offer to rub them for you if I know you better."

"Oh, please offer, señor. I would be most happy." With that, she moved closer and put her foot on one of his legs. "Grazie, grazie. I am called Ashlina. How about you?"

"Garrett," he uttered, "Garrett LaPearl."

"Lovely. You may start rubbing now."

"Oh yes, forgive me." Truth be told, Garrett was so captured by her beauty, he forgot what she wanted for a moment. He took her foot in both hands and began rubbing her feet. A few times he stroked her soles with his fingernails, and she began to giggle.

"I am quite ticklish, but I love it just the same." She seemed to be purring like a cat as he continued.

Hoon Kim sat on the mahogany stool in the Imperial Hotel lounge, downtown Saigon. It was two o'clock in the afternoon, and Kim was dressed to kill. He wore a cream-colored Pierre Cardin suit, black tie, hand painted only, by choice. The silk black shirt was lightly starched. His shoes were Gucci. Now and then, his gold Rolex would show its diamond-encrusted face on his left wrist.

Born in South Korea, Hoon Kim was the son of a wealthy diplomat. His holdings were both legal and some on the other side of the law. In the eyes of the authorities whom he paid a great deal of money, his record was squeaky clean. Beyond the law was an understatement. Kim Senior owned many hotels throughout the world. His business included several banks, an oil company in South America, several major newspapers, and the list goes on and on. Hoon Jr. was the undisputed heir, apparently the only true benefactor. Hoon the father's connections reached, some say, all the way to the highest government seats in Korea. Hoon Jr. was directly in charge of every illegal activity throughout the world. Their main source of income, which were staggering amounts, come from the lucrative heroin trade. The family owned thousands of acres of poppy throughout Asia, Cambodia being the most productive. The Kim family built makeshift factories throughout the jungles of Vietnam, Laos, and Cambodia. The revenues the drug brought in were staggering. Estimates ranged from five billion to fifty billion every year. Their tentacles reached out as far away as Los Angeles, New York, and Honolulu.

Seemingly an impenetrable empire, Hoon Kim Jr. ran a very tight ship and did not spare the rod. Workers mysteriously disappeared without a trace. Executions were common. Kim believed in taking no prisoners. On a whim, he would have one of his loyal henchmen cut out someone's tongue simply if he suspected a betrayal. The majority of the workers were deathly afraid of Hoon Kim. Because of their impoverished living conditions and lack of money, most said nothing and remained loyal. Kim was one of the major drug lords who paid more than the average wage, enough to keep them away from his competitors. Kim hated the term *drug dealer*; he preferred to be called simply a *king*.

Kim Jr. was also very friendly with remnants of the

Khmer Rouge, arguably the deadliest and most ruthless despots in all of Asia and Africa. Kim hired them to protect his empire. This protection insulated his world from the outside. The Khmer Rouge were truly a killing machine. Kim was usually accompanied by a small army of his most trusted soldiers whenever he traveled. Occasionally, when away on business, Kim would play a game of hide and seek with his bodyguards. Typically, he would sneak away, find himself a high-priced call girl, and spend the night in one of the rooms of his hotel, driving his bodyguards up a wall.

# "THE SECOND TIME"

"Anastasia has been recovering from her first assignment for two weeks now," said Sir Nigel. "It's time to go back to work."

Killing Thomas Mark had taken its toll on Nasta. Three days after the assassination, she was puking her guts up. She was depressed and wretched with guilt and anxiety.

"Get over it," bellowed Sir Nigel. "You and I have work to do. Get on with it. Snap out of it, things will get easier as time goes on. This time next year, you'll have killed at least twenty of these scumbags. The world will rejoice, and you will be a lord, except no one will know who you are." Nigel let out a huge belly laugh that shook the room.

# ROME

"That is pretty much my whole day, the shortened version," he chuckled. "It was a little too crazy for my taste, but then again, that's what creators are for, I guess."

"This Ms. Graffo, does she have a first name?" said his mother.

"I believe it is Ashlina or Altina," he paused, "something like that."

"Well, are you or aren't you?" Fiona inquired. "Come on, spit it out."

"Am I what, Mother?"

"You know, in love, dummy. Are you in love with this young siren? Tell your mother. This is Rome, perhaps the most romantic city in the world. What a great place to lose your virginity, wouldn't you agree?" laughed Fiona. "That glow in your face isn't there for nothing. I think I have answered my own questions. Perhaps Ashlina feels the very same way."

"I don't think so, given the fact she ran off into the night with that Jackson fellow." Uttering the sentence again about Ashlina willingly absconding the situation made Garrett sick to his stomach. "I thought I was safe with her, and all of a sudden, this freakin' master stud right out of a Banana Republic photo shoot appears out of nowhere."

Garrett went to his bed and dove on it as if it were a swimming pool like he used to do while participating on the Haddon Hills diving team when he was seventeen. He was known for his perfect jackknife and half gainers. As his head struck the firm Sleep Number bed, he quickly came back to reality without a splash. Half naked, Garrett lay on the antique brass bed and reflected on the day's adventures. *All in all, a wild day*, he thought. *I didn't get the girl, but almost.* The room was perfectly silent, except for his mother's heavy breathing when suddenly Garrett heard a faint tap on the door. *Just my imagination,* he thought, *who could it be?* Then suddenly, he heard it again. This time, it was accompanied by a slight moan, the kind when someone is scared. *There it is again!* With that, Garrett leaped out of bed and rushed to the door. There, sitting on the floor, in the same clothes was Ms. Ashlina Graffo. She was rolled up in a ball.

"Please help me, Garrett, please." Those words coming from her beautiful mouth, although troubled, were music to his ears. Garrett found himself staring at the young beauty, but quickly snapped back to reality.

"Forgive me, come in, come in. Make yourself comfortable."

With that, Ashlina leaped up on the antique couch and stretched out.

"What the hell happened?"

"I will tell you everything, but first, can I have a drink of any alcohol that you may have?"

"But of course, how about a glass of Nocello or Sambuca, you tell me," retorted Garrett.

"Nocello sounds good." Garrett poured her a small glass and sat down at the far end of the sofa.

"Please, now tell me what has happened."

"First, I have a confession to make. I am not just your ordinary, run-of-the-mill, beautiful, intelligent, funny, not—"

"Okay, I get it, modesty is not included with the superlatives," chuckled Garrett. "Go on."

"Well, like I have told you, my name is Ashlina Graffo, you may call me Ash, and I chose to stay at the particular hotel for a simple reason."

What? said Garrett.

"Because my father," she paused a little, "Yes, my daddy owns it, along with twenty-five others all over the world."

"Whatttt?" yelled Garrett. "Your father must have money coming out of his nose," quipped Garrett.

"I am afraid so," said Ash. "I am afraid so."

"Why are you so sheepish about it?"

"Because it is a pain in the ass. You see, I actually have bodyguards nearby, 24-7, and tonight, for the first time, I gave them the slip. I actually paid your friend Mr. D. something like two hundred American dollars to help me pull it off. He was great. D'Amberville, that was his name. Then you appeared just at the right time, and my plan worked to perfection. We flushed you out and you were the other white knight, along with the paid accomplice. Garrett, somebody tried to kill me out there. That was no accident. I am scared to death. You see, my father is a very powerful man and sits in a position of prominence in the Sicilian Mafia."

"Holy shit, Ash, my father was a gangster as well until

he was gunned down not too long ago. He got whacked one night in our home, holy shit."

"Well, what are we going to do now, Gar?"

"I don't know as of this moment, but I'll tell you one thing, we are not going to make it easy on these people, whoever they are. We must get out of this hotel. They probably know where we are staying by now. I will fill my mother in while you collect your things, and we'll meet by the cabstand right out front."

"Isn't that a little too conspicuous" said Ash.

"Well, if you allow me to finish, I'll tell you the rest."

Ash giggled, "I am very spoiled, you see, and used to getting my way."

"I will pay three people to wear our coats and pretend they are getting in the taxi, and we will slip out of the back of the building and escape whoever is watching, and we will head outside of the city. My mother and I have cousins all over Italy."

"Sounds like a plan," said Ash. Suddenly, there was a loud explosion.

# ENGLAND

"Two weeks have gone by, and I'm still not over it." Nasta had worried look on her face when she heard a knock on her door. "Who is it?" she asked. "I wish to be alone."

A key could be heard sliding into the keyhole and she stepped back. "Don't you know by now that I have a key to every room in the house?" mused Nigel.

"I forgot," chuckled Nasta. "What can I do for you?"

Nigel handed Nasta a copy of the *London Times* and told her to look at the front page. There, right on the front page, was a picture of Thomas Mark, the man she had assassinated.

"Holy shit, what is going on?"

"Read the article, the authorities believe they have the murder suspect, when lo and behold, she is standing right here."

"How did you—"

"Well, I arranged someone else to take the fall, and you are as free as a bird."

"Clever, Nigel, clever. You old fart!" They both broke out in a hearty laugh.

Nasta awoke the next day with seemingly a little extra bounce in her step. She had achieved a goal, one that is totally out of the ordinary and got away with it free and clean. She is no different than any other corporate executive that is on the rise. *What a freakin' night*, she thought. What a high. All the newspapers in the major cities were doting on this killer who had so suddenly burst on the scene. The Black Rose, dubbed as such because it left a black rose at its scene of the murder. Although it really does not exist, the popular flower lends itself to the situation indeed. *I must get more this time and give the world the dramas they desire.*

The assignment came about a month later, the usual procedure—a manila envelope slid under her bedroom door. This time it was much the deer ardent especially said, "Do Not Bend." Nasta bent down and picked up the envelope and placed it on the four poster bed. Nigel spared no expense when it came to furnishings. She broke its seal and began to examine the photographs, about twenty of them. The main person in the pictures was truly one creepy-looking individual. Up at the top left hand corner was his name, birth date, etc. His name is Hoon Kim. His dossier read like a who's who of international crime-log—murder, drug running, slavery, prostitutes, drug laboratories in the middle of the jungles of Vietnam, Cambodia, and Laos. He insulated his empire as best he could. But on that scale, it was exceedingly different.

"Where are you, sweetheart?" questioned his wife Onee. "I feel like I haven't seen you in weeks, lover. Let's spend some time together today, pleassssseee. Your business can wait, can't it? Did you marry me or your business? I'll tell Daddy to change the will," she laughed. "Oh he would not come?"

"I am his only son. I am a lad spoiled," as he glided past a full-length mirrors and snided. *My, my, I am nice to look at*, he thought.

"Yes, you are, dear," knowing exactly what he was thinking. Onee Kim was like no other when it came to finances. Her father, Tiko Yamada, was a very wealthy Japanese oil and real estate tycoon. He was recently listed as one of the top ten richest men in the world, according to *Forbes Magazine*. Once he was absolutely shining. Half Japanese and half Korean simply produced gorgeous offspring.

"Gorgeous, I will not stay out too long," he promised. He whipped out his black cell phone to summon his driver and bodyguards who were with him 24-7.

"I cannot wait to try out this new weapon," Nasta said with quite a gleam in her eye. The weapon she referred to was a high-powered scoped rifle made exclusively by Russian gun makers. This modern masterpiece was very rare. It is said that there were only ten like it in the world. A former Nazi hunter, a Jew named Issac Mendel, had ordered the shipment fifteen years ago, but somehow Mendel had emphatically disappeared, believed to have been taken out by the Gestapo as he became more than an insurance. The gun was designed to be extremely accurate up to one and a half miles away. It only weighs about eight pounds, so it was very easy to transport. This model could be disassembled into six pieces in a matter of minutes.

The price tag had been left on the trigger, obviously a joke by Nigel. The gun had been handcrafted by a Russian gunman in Munich. His store there is a front for the Russian mob. Each piece started at twenty-five thousand American dollars. The gunman knew not to ask any questions as he was rewarded handsomely by the Kim family. No slipups, everything had to be perfect, or he would end up floating in the river. It was said that the gun maker would create these rifles for some of the most ruthless militants in the world—the Khmer Rouge, the yakuza to name a few.

Nasta, on this assignment, was allowed to hire an accomplice. After looking at hundreds of pages of photographs of guns for hire, she stopped at the photo of one Robito, Sanchez Manuel. Robito stood six feet two inches tall with solid muscle and wide girth. He was, in simplest terms, a mercenary, a hired gun, a stone-cold killer. Some say that he doesn't even exist. Nasta liked his long gray hair and beard. But he was also a master of disguises. He could blend into any situation that no one has ever given a full description of this man. He was born outside of Sydney, a true Aussie. His family moved around quite a bit, finally settling in Bolivia in the pampas, home of the gauchos.

The file of Mr. Etlaw combined an untraceable phone number where he could always be reached. Only about ten people had this number in the entire world. Mr. Etlaw was very cautious and highly trained. According to record, as of this listing, he has never been wounded or even scratched up until this point.

This meeting was set for 5:00 p.m. on Friday the 15 of September. Nasta was given explicit directions where to meet this man. At the corner of Holden Street and Lucas Boulevard was a small well-kept park right in the middle of Piccadilly. People seemed to go there to meditate or gather their thoughts. Everyone minded their own business and went about their way. The Holden Street pub did a brisk business located on the corner. Nasta was very nervous as the palms of her hands grew moist with perspiration. The park was empty except for a few people, maybe ten at the most. The smell of fall away in the air, and also was the smell of danger. As she entered the park, she looked around for an older man with gray hair and probably reading a book.

Yesterday, she received by courier at the compound an audio cassette with a strange female voice giving specific instructions to Nasta about this rendezvous. "They could have waited a little longer," she quipped to herself, laced with sarcasm. "I mean, today is Friday, and they just sent the tape yesterday. Oh well, I—"

Suddenly, out of nowhere, three men dressed in black ninja-like clothing ran into the park and opened fire with automatic weapons and commenced firing on someone sitting on a bench. In a matter of minutes, the man was dead from what she could see from where she was standing. The gunmen took a quick look around and were then picked up by a black sedan with tinted glass. It happened so fast; Nasta was very lucky to have been concealed by a large fir bush or the killer may have turned on her as well. She quickly raced across the street and dashed into the pub as the sound of police sirens could be heard in the distance. *Thank God that I was cautious*, she thought. *I could have gotten hit in the crossfire. Holy shit*! She ordered a pint of stout and blended into her surroundings. The police arrived along with an ambulance. People were running everywhere, trying to get out of the area. Nasta was always taught to be quick, but not in a hurry. She was the Black Rose; nobody could kill her—nobody. For a few moments, she had forgotten about Mr. Etlaw.

*He must have been the person who was shot, oh my god.* As she finished her beer, another code in her training, she was instructed to wait for a phone call from Nigel across the street in a phone booth. The instructions read like this: "Pick up the ringing phone and drop it after only one ring. Walk one block north, and you will receive a call on your portable phone."

As she reached her point, her phone rang, and the voice of Nigel became audible. He said, "The wrong man was killed, do not become alarmed. Get out of the area. And get on the tube and head south to Trafalgar Square. There, a green Mercedes will pick you up. Act like a tourist! Look up at the tall buildings and sigh out loud like you were amazed at the architecture of some of the buildings, act like a tourist!"

The hotel room cost six pounds, roughly forty-five American dollars. It contained one bed, a small bathroom, and a great view of the park, the perfect vantage point. The man could scan the entire area and watch the comings and goings of every pedestrian entering or leaving the park. Mr. Etlaw had become suspicious a week ago when a courier arrived at the hotel with his instructions. Every detail, except for one slight addition—the black Mercedes. If they were terrorists, they were not very good. Mr. Etlaw knew it was a setup. The man called Nigel, with whom they had worked for many, many times would never betray him, but the young girl, who was she? As Mr. Etlaw peered out of the windows, standing a few feet from the window and using a high-powered telescope, the shrill ring coming from his secure phone startled him for a few seconds.

"Hello, this is Batman, what the fuck happened?"

"We don't know," muttered Nigel. "We think it was a bunch of expatriates from Albania that would love to put you down and collect that evergrowing bounty on your head."

"Very funny, Nigel, old boy, very fuckin' funny. But who was it? One of yours?"

"Oui," Nigel answered in French, an attempt to lighten the moment. "She is new, but not to be underestimated. She is the Black Rose, perhaps you have heard of her." Etlaw's face turned ashen gray, and he began to stutter, an old impediment he had as a child and still experiences at when he becomes nervous. "She is the new rising star," said Nigel with a hint of cockiness. "She is my latest masterpiece. Okay, what next, old boy?"

Nasta, stretched out on her bed back at the school, her mind racing, but her body totally relaxed, a desired trait for this love of work. She had kicked off her Gucci shoes, with crepe soles and waited for Nigel's return. Someone knocked softly on her door, and she knew at once it was Nigel.

"I am so sorry about the incident at the park, it could not be helped. That is why—" A large man with jet-black hair stylishly trimmed walked into her room without an announcement and smiled. "This is Mr. Etlaw, Nasta. At least I think it is," laughed Nigel.

"Having read your file ten times, I am truly honored, Mr. Etlaw, truly."

"No, the honor is mine, your reputation precedes you."

"Meeee, I did not know," Nasta said innocently.

"Believe it or not, Ms. Nasta, there is actually quite a few of us assassins out there," retorted Etlaw. "We simply do not know and very few choose to be a ghost," chuckled Etlaw.

Nasta was very excited, and like it was no time, she leaped off the bed like a cheetah ready to kill. "Wait here a moment, Mr. Etlaw. I wish to show you something. Please wait!" She quickly left the room and entered the large parlor area. Two minutes later, she reentered the bedroom and said, "Where is Mr. Etlaw?" Nigel had relieved himself in the bathroom, and that quickly, he left Nigel and Nasta, standing there completely bewildered.

"The beat goes on, my dear, the beat goes on."

As Etlaw pressed the button to retire in his first-class bed-like seat, he pondered for a moment about the young assassin/heroine. People make choices in this crazy world for whatever reason or reasons. And this young lady quickly has become very famous and respected in various strata of life. This one, the one they call the Black Rose, shall have another day to kill again.

# (A RINA DECO)

The next day, Garrett and Fiona rose early, ate their typical continental breakfast, and hailed a taxi heading to the airport. Neither was in a talkative mood, the events that took place this and last week had taken their toll on them both. Garrett stole a glance at his dozing mother and thought, *Thank God we made it out of this crazy city alive. Yes, dear, thank God.* Garrett had the window seat in first class and liked to look at his previous destination when suddenly, there right out near the runway stood Ashlina Graffo with her two huge bodyguards. She was waving and jumping up and down. Somehow she knew Garrett was on that plane, in that seat. *Wow, what a woman, what a crazy woman.*

As the plane took off and disappeared into the clouds, Ashlina thought about the time she had spent with the handsome stranger. He had truly affected her life. It was a special feeling like no other. Perhaps, for the very first time, she was falling in love. Bruno, the larger of the two gorilla-like bodyguards stood by her side, looking for an enemy, simply doing his job. Ashlina glanced up and smiled and was thankful for what she had.

# LONDON

Jackson D'Amberville strolled down the main thoroughfares of London as if he designed them himself.

He couldn't care less if he got lost. If indeed he did, he would simply stop at the nearest pub and raise a few pints. He continued to flip his gold dollar piece so incessantly that his nail on his flip finger had become chipped and a slight trickle of blood appeared. To Jackson, this was a good thing because, just like a shark, the smell of blood would attract the human sharks—women! Women from all over the world were out on this pleasant spring evening, and D'Amberville was in his element. Orientals, Italians, French walking by—some noticing his unusual habit and others simply content to smile back at the attractive stranger. Jackson was on the prowl, and he loved it. A large chauffer-driven vehicle double parked in front of the Sterling Palladium pulled out and nearly hit Jack on the leg. "What a JO," uttered Jack. *The hoi polloi I suppose, a bunch of idiots*, he thought. *No regard for other people.*

Sigmund Jeffries drove the black limo with great comfort and ease. He was used to the type of ride it provided. Having grown up in Yorkshire, he was raised by his father in the estate house of a rather large property. The land and house were owned by a wealthy businessman who liked to be driven to work in a limo every day. This night, he was paid sixty quid to perform the service of scaring this rather slave of society, Jackson D., by coming close to hitting Jack's leg with his vehicle. He was told to simply scare him, which would quickly turn to anger. Sigmund chuckled and said to himself, "I feel like I am in a spy movie or something," wondering again "who was that well-dressed guy who paid me sixty quick to do such a mundane task. Oh well, better not to ask any questions. That guy there was something strange, something scary about him. Best to mind my own business."

Jackson's instincts were right on—sorry indeed.

# ASHLINA

The plane ride from Rome's airport was nothing out the ordinary. The food was fifty-fifty, and the turbulence had little to no effect on the comfort of the flight as she sat in her first-class recliner. And of course, she sat nearest to the window without asking since her father actually owned the airlines.

"I can't stop thinking about him," she whispered to herself. "This is way too complicated, way too icky for me. I feel like if someone doesn't tell me exactly where he is right now, I will go crazy, absolutely nutso." She began to laugh uncontrollably, louder, louder until Ash finally let out her last guffaw; her stomach was killing her. The flight crew laughed along with her, politely, but as soon as she turned her head, they all looked at one another, rolled their eyes, and left the cabin, shaking their heads. Ashlina was a show unto herself.

Garrett was just drifting off to sleep when suddenly his mother jumped up out of sound sleep and let out a scream that could have woken the dead. "It's okay, Mother, you're safe with me. No one can touch you, you're safe, on the way home to the good old USA."

Fiona and Garrett decided to fly home first class and it was great. Plenty of food and drink, with great service—just what they both needed. The plane ride back was very nice except for a few really bad turbulences, unusually bad, but not for long. Suddenly, the plane began to rise and fall once again. Garrett started feeling a little sick, the magazine he was reading dropped to the floor. He looked over at his mother who was fast asleep, peaceful and unknowing of the danger that was just ahead. Two men dressed in Brioni suits and Gucci shoes got up from their first-class seats and, in a matter of seconds, brandished two handguns and pointed them directly at Fiona!

"Don't do anything stupid, my Italian Pisano, or I will blow her brains out right here. We made sure that our people in Italy put us on the safest plane in the sky. All compartments are bulletproof so if somebody fired a weapon, the plane would not decompress! Yep, you, my friend, will be our mouthpiece to the pilots, and you will take us where we want to go, so just sit there and shut the fuck up! Ya hear me, Pisano?"

Fiona stirred and started to fall back to sleep when the criminal scud woke her up. "Now, we surely don't want her to miss any of the fun." With that, they both broke out laughing. "Tell her to get up."

Ashlina's rerouted flight was wonderful; she took her father's personal pilot to follow the same flight plan as the 747 that left the airport just ahead of the Graffo personal jet. *Perhaps I will bump into him on purpose, and we will embrace and live happily ever after. Be real,* her inner voice said to her, *don't be such a dreamer.*

The two gunners seemed to grow more and more nervous, seemingly waiting for something to happen. Nobody but the hijackers knew anything. The plane was starting its descent, where would it land, no one knew. "Holy shit," Garrett whispered to his mother. "Excuse, my friend. But where the fuck are we?" The gunners were very steady, well-framed for sure. Mario, the older was looked over at Garrett and began to chuckle.

"We know you, little man. We tried to whack your father a couple times, but he was too clever, but he made mistakes, he was human. He's lucky he got shot, lucky we didn't grab him hard off the streets. I would have shown him my little blowtorch."

"You mothafuckers, you killed my father."

"That's right, Pisano, it was I. Mario has assisted my men, there was nothing he could do, but I always liked your pops, he taught me a lot." Garrett could feel his insides ready to burst right out of his body. *I want to kill them both*, but he couldn't because they had his mother tied up and gagged. Garrett had to wait for the right moment. "We are almost on the ground and our work here will be over. Did you know by now that we are hired hits out of Chicago, little man?"

"No, I didn't."

"Shut up, Laslow. Shut the fuck up, Mario. He is as good as dead."

Nasta was strolling the airport when she spotted a plane getting ready to land, but there were no lights to guide them in, and it appeared as though the plane was trying to shake on to the landing site. *Very unusual,* she thought. *I wonder if something weird is happening, I wonder.*

She waited another ten minutes before heading toward the large Cessna craft, which was now fully grounded. Nasta, being the smart one, was carrying a large hunting knife strapped to her leg and a Walther PPK, a brand-new gun, which was introduced to the world in Germany a few weeks ago. The design was smaller, almost able to disappear in a large person's hand, but still very effective at close range. Nasta loved this handgun as she affectionately referred to it as "my little pistola." As she walked across the tarmac toward the Cessna, she could hear a conversation coming from the plane. Someone had smartly opened a window in row sixteen, seat D, a window seat. Some of the talk was in another language. *Italian, definitely,* she thought, *which could make this situation much less complicated. I can kill these two morons, and nobody will ever know or care. Hired hits from Sicily, I would guess.*

Suddenly, there was movement on the plane. Nasta could hear someone shouting, "Sit down, sit down you piece of shit, and you too, lady," referring to Fiona, "sit the fuck down."

Just then, Nasta saw one of the men leave the plane,

heading toward a black limo that was parked about two hundred yards away. He was probably checking out the situation, making sure there were no complications. *The perfect opportunity, now is the time,* she thought. With that, she sprinted across the fifty feet or so of pavement just the way she was taught to run. As a bird trying to elude her captors, she was extremely fast. She made it without being seen in seconds flat and hid under the left wing where she was fortunate enough to see one of the gunmen with his back to the window. *The right moment to slip onto the plane and kill this man who held the four captive.* Screwing her silencer on the Walther took exactly fifteen seconds, just the way she trained for this situation, back in England. Just then, the main door of the plane flew open and neatly dropped to the ground. Headcount four—she calculated three civilians and one crackpot, Americans perhaps. The male assailant did not know what hit him as he walked down the portable stairs. Nasta was about ten feet away as she tossed the knife she carried directly at the man. Her weapon found its mark; she bent over the fallen man to examine her handiwork and retrieve her knife. And when the other three ran into the waiting area, she reached into her inside pocket, gently sliding a black rose out of her leather jacket. *I may as well take the credit.* She chuckled. *I believe I accidently did something good.*

Back in England, Nigel paced the floor in his study, wondering how Nasta was doing on this assignment. He felt, with all the training so far, that she would be able to handle any situation, but one never knows sometimes, especially when you were young and aggressive. *I always told her to be quick, but never in a hurry.* Nigel had read that in a book some years back about an American basketball coach. *Good stuff*, he thought to himself.

Suddenly, the telephone rang, and Nigel raced toward it, the secure line, and picked it up. Nigel could hear the sound of heavy breathing and then silence. Since it was a secure line, he could say her name out loud.

"Nasta, where are you?"

"At the airport and I am safe."

"Thank God," he said.

"Barely," Nasta replied. "Just barely."

"What do you mean just barely?"

"Well, I followed a hunch and got caught in a crunch," she giggled. "But I was armed and prepared, so I am okay."

"Where are you?"

"Don't ask," she muttered. "Don't ask."

Nigel hung up with slight trepidation, but more at ease, just the same.

Ashlina was exhausted after the hijacking and decided to call it a night. *Somehow I will find this kinky American and live happily ever after. At least for a couple of months anyway.* She got back into the safety of the bulletproof limo which the Graffo family kept at several different airports throughout the world just in case. Ash was delighted to get off her feet and find a hotel and then proceed to New York in the morning.

Meanwhile, Garrett and Fiona were rebooked to another flight to New York with arrival time of 9:15 a.m. The buzz from the engines began to put Garrett to sleep, although he really wanted to keep an eye on his mother. She had fallen asleep already in their first-class accommodations. The seats were extremely soft, perfect for snoozing. Fiona was talking in her sleep, mumbling something about Rocco. He stared at her lovely sleeping face and thought that she had been through so much. Later, even though they planned on staying longer, they had to get back to New Jersey.

# ROBERT ETLAW

Robert Etlaw remained in London for the next few days, hoping to run into the Black Rose again. Even though he had been loyal to Nigel over the years, he really was loyal to only one thing and one thing only, and that was money. Word on the street was that there was bounty on the Black Rose worth quite a bit of money—5 million, starting at 3.5 million American. To his knowledge the highest sum ever offered on one person.

*I wonder who is backing this hit*, thought Etlaw. *I just wonder. With her recent kills, the international community is getting pissed off at her choices for economic reasons. She must be stopped. Nigel can never know that I cater to both sides of the fence. I made the mistake of telling him years ago about my thousand-acre farm in Bolivia, where my wife and three children live. Nigel would send a hit squat, and within hours they would all be killed.*

"One more job, that's all," Etlaw said aloud. "Just one more and with that amount I could retire and spend more time with my family. How could I pull it off? It has to be perfect, with the perfect patsy, think! Think."

Robert Etlaw lived a relatively simple existence, besides being a gun for hire. The most contracts in a year that he would take would be ten, ranging from a warlord in Niger who was slowing down the diamond trade to a politician in Brazil that was getting greedy. He was born in Bowling Green, Ohio, the son of Mabel and Ettanggar. Sam was a union worker and Mabel was the executive assistant to the president of the local bank. They actually resided in a small town thirty miles south of Bowling Green. Bob, as he was called in his hometown as a kid, was sixteen years old when he decided to steal a car and was dumb enough to get caught. When it was time for his trial, he decided to skip town, to see the world outside of Bowling Green, Ohio. For the next forty years, he became Robert Etlaw a.k.a. Robert M. Ettanggar. One day while daydreaming, lying in the sun, Robert calculated he had visited forty cities around the world, and by the time he was twenty-one years young, he had killed his first mark. The contract totaled one hundred dollars. *I wish that I had never gotten involved in this business. Yeah, I wouldn't have nearly the amount of money accumulated, but maybe I would be happy living a normal life.*

Forty years later, Etlaw was sitting in an English pub in London, England. *I will kill this Black Rose and collect the bounty. I could have killed her the other day, but that would have been too easy.* Assassins really enjoyed the chase, hunting and stalking their prey and called it professional pride. *Next time, young lady, you will help me retire.* Etlaw could not stop thinking of Nasta. She became an uninvited guest in his mind on a regular basis. Etlaw had never experienced anything like this before. Perhaps he had encountered her before. After all, London was a huge city, but one never knows.

Friday, hot day in June, summer in England, Nasta made her way back to the compound. She could not wait to take a long hot shower and try to forget about today's incidences for a while. Lately, she has caught herself looking in the mirror more than ever, admiring her chiseled cheekbones, her muscular figure, and her well-coifed hair. *Yes,* she thought.

*I've come a long way from my humble beginnings. Slovenia is a long way indeed.* A soft knock in her bedroom door startled her, causing her to bump her head on the bedpost. From the high Showa pillow, she saw the manila envelope sliding under the thick oak bedroom door. Her next assignment. She was hoping to take a few days off to be a regular person for a short while, but Nigel was relentless. He never seemed to rest. He would often say "Rest is for the rest, death goes on." Nasta began opening the envelope and noticed that her left hand was trembling a bit. Perhaps this one was the most challenging thus far. With that, she closed her eyes and fell into a deep sleep.

# HADDON HILLS, NEW JERSEY

Garrett and Fiona arrived in New Jersey Monday morning at 8:30 a.m. in JFK Airport, New York. The city was absolutely crazy on a Monday morning, right in the middle of rush hour. Garrett had planned it this way. His logic told him that they could hide easier and get lost in the crowds if in fact there was a contract out on him and his mother. *Unbelievable,* he thought to himself, *fucking unbelievable. If we could just slip through the airport and get my mother to one of my father's apartments that he would use as his safe houses in case a war broke out.* Rocco never told other wiseguys about these places. He trusted no one.

The first safe house they came to was in Queens, smack-dab in the middle of the largest Greek population in the city. The streets were alive with traffic, both walking pedestrians and vehicles. In this part of Queens, they say a person could hide for a month without being found; it was perfect. Fiona could catch up on some reading, one of her favorite pastimes, and Garrett could simply think about where and how to escape and plan their next course of action.

"What would my father do?" he said to himself. He needed advice and he knew it. Suddenly he had a thought. He recalled his father saying to him as a teenager, "When you get in trouble or need some help, call Sartouk. Call Sartouk and he will come right away, his loyalty to me knows no bounds." Apparently, Rocco had taken Sartouk under his wing when he was a young boy. He adopted him, but not in the legal sense; wiseguys didn't work that way. No paperwork per se, but binding nonetheless. Rocco cut Sartouk loose when he was eighteen. Presently, at age twenty-five, Sartouk is running an electric appliance supply store in south Philly, basically a front for fenced items and a major moneymaker in the black market for the mob. Theodore Sartouk. Garrett recalled quickly where he kept his phone number and where he lived in South Philadelphia.

As he approached the bedroom of this safe house, he remembered that the safe Rocco kept valuables in was actually part of a light fixture in the bathroom. Garrett stepped up on a stool and retrieved the information. There, inside the safe, neatly folded, was the info he needed—310 Darien Street was the address along with his phone number.

"Hello," the voice on the other side answered the phone. He sounded a bit groggy, but after all, it was two o'clock in the morning.

# PHILLY

"Yoooh, what's happening, little man?" Theodore Sartouk always reminded Garrett that he was the first son of Rocco LaPearl. "Long time no see, what can I do for you?" Sartouk knew right away there was danger. This telephone number was known only to himself, Rocco, and now Garrett.

"I'm holed up in New York, in a safe house. Just got back into the US from Italy. I heard that there is a hit out for me and my mother. Is that true, T?"

"Yeah, I'm afraid it's true. Those m'fers believe that you know too much, including your mother. For now, sit tight. I'll look into this problem for you. Your father has a couple of guns tucked away in that house, arm yourself and be very careful. Trust no one except me. You know what I mean?"

"Are you still repeating that one hundred times a day?" They both laughed.

"You know what I mean."

Everyone in South Camden knew that T. Sartouk repeated himself hundreds of times in conversation, repeating the phrase "You know what I mean," but no one had the balls to say it to his face.

When Sartouk got the word from Garrett, he quickly hit the streets to find out who put out the hit. His first source would be Joey Scungill, a long time mob associate who has been selling into to the mob for years. Sartouk found him on Second and Mifflin, sitting on the corner, seemingly watching traffic go by, both human and auto. Sartouk drove a black late-model Caddy, a typical wiseguy car. T. guided his car right up to Joey and almost took his foot off.

"Ah oh, trouble." Before Joey could conjure up an escape, Sartouk was all over him. T. Sartouk was quite the football player in high school, a running back, built life in a refrigerator.

"Get in, Joey, nowwww!"

"Sure, T., anything you say."

"Just get in here and don't worry. I'm not going to whack you. You know what I mean." Sartouk smiled as he looked in the rearview mirror at Joey sweating like a pig. T. burst out laughing at the sight of Joey squirming in the backseat.

"Okay, Joey, lay it on me. Who really wanted this done so bad that he or they didn't care who knew it?"

"It was sanctioned by the Reginello family, originally out of New York."

"I know, I know, ya douche bag. Who carried out this piece of work, Joey, ya jerk off?"

"It was a wiseguy out of the Bronx, black something or other. That's all I know. I swear, T., on my mother's soul."

"Okay, get the fuck out of my car now!"

Sartouk had heard the same rumor on the streets. If Joey said the same thing, then usually you could make book on it.

As he hung up the phone, Garrett had a sinister, beguiling look on his face. Earlier that night, he had gotten the call from Sartouk. He now knew what to do to avenge the death of his father. As he lay stretched out on the featherbed, he began to plan out his revenge—a dish enjoyed most when it was cold. The other side of his brain was concentrating strictly on the young lady that was stealing his heart. *Ohhh, Ashlina Graffo, where are you now?*

"Excuse me, scusa, señor, can you please tell me how far Haddon Hills is?" Ashlina had taken a shuttle, a puddle jumper, simply a very small plane late last night to follow a hunch that Garrett lived there. While in Rome, she had heard him talk about his hometown.

The airport worker responded, "About ninety miles, ma'am." Observing her fine clothing and jewelry, a small-faced Rolex, silk blouse, and three-hundred-dollar shoes, his girlfriend is a budding designer in New York, so he knew what he was talking about. Ashlina was dressed to kill and take a few prisoners in the process. *I'll probably take one of those airport shuttles to New Jersey, money is no object*, she thought to herself.

As Ashlina proceeded to the runway to board the same plane, she noticed that a group of about ten people began to gather directly below the loading truck to take the passengers directly out to the plane. It was then that she realized that she stood about ten yards away from Garrett, Garrett LaPearl. *It had to be him, it just had to be. Talk about luck*, she thought. *No, no, no, this had to be fate or even karma. He has to recognize me, this is too good to be true. Call out to him,* her inner voice cried. *Do not let him slip away again!* Just then her voice became incessantly loud. "Garrett, oh my dearest Garrett," but something terrible beyond words happened. When the man turned around, it clearly was not Garrett, an impostor perhaps, a mere coincidence. "No, it can't be." Just then, shots rang out. *Where? Over there.*

Suddenly, Ashlina felt someone's hand grab her arm and yank her away from everyone else. That same hand cupped their fingers over her mouth so she couldn't scream. Tears had welled up in her eyes, her vision impaired. As the tears began to dry, her vision restored, "Oh my god in heaven. First you were over there, now here. No, it couldn't be. You-he-no—yess, yess, yess, it is you."

"Yes, my dear lady, the other man is my double, my lookalike. We are in great danger. There is what the Sicilians call a contract, a hit on my life, so Umberto pretended he was me and my mother so I can slip away safely, capisce?"

"Yes, I think so, and what about Umberto?"

"Ah, don't worry about him. He is a trained killer, a weapons expert like no other, and a tenth degree black belt. Come now," implored Garrett. "Let us get to our house while we still can."

"Anything you say, Garrett, anything. It is so good to see you."

A long black Mercedes was waiting for them, and they were whisked away from the bright lights of the airport.

The ride from the airport took about an hour and a half. Of course he was given explicit directions to lose any possible bad guys trying to follow Garrett's vehicle. Johann B., Garrett's bodyguard and driver, was an expert driver. Ashlina was fast asleep in the backseat along with Fiona. Both were completely wiped out from the day's events. Garrett was riding shotgun. A position he normally wouldn't find himself in. His father always made him ride in the back as a young man, taking every precaution; that was the life he lived. When they pulled up to the safe house, this one was different; all the lights were off.

"Johnnie, go on ahead and check the house before the girls and I go in."

"Sure thing, boss," as if he was addressing Rocco.

"You can call me Garrett, Johnnie. My father is dead."

"Sure thing, Bbbb . . ."—nervous cough—"Garrett. I'll check the house."

*A lotta brawn, but not much brain*, thought Garrett, *not much.*

After he thoroughly checked the safe house, he came back to the car to escort the two ladies in. They both were very difficult to wake up.

"Ahhhh, where are we?"

"Safe," said Garrett. "Please go in and make yourself comfortable."

Robert Etlaw moved with ease in London. Having been there about a hundred times over the years, he knew every back-alley and started for a way to quickly escape. As he approached his rendezvous with the Black Rose, he kept thinking strange thoughts about this young girl. First of all, he could easily put one in the back of her pretty head and collect the reward. No, no, he couldn't do that to Nigel, his old confidant. *Noooo, or maybe . . .* That thought had to be put to rest.

Nasta approached the old garage on Chauncey Street with great caution. She was wearing her night clothes, including her crepe-soled shoes. After all, she really didn't know Mr. Etlaw that well. She had checked her weapon of choice—a small, but deadly knife, small enough to conceal in her palm. It was dipped in a curare, death coming five minutes after piercing the victim's skin, giving Nasta plenty of time to escape and leaving her ID, the black rose, with Etlaw watching her back. A simple job indeed, but quite daring just the same. This job required her to make the hit in a crowded theater. The Belvedere was across the street from the garage. They had agreed to meet there for last minute directions. Nasta would be wearing a Donna Karan silk blouse and silk trousers and four-inch heels, not her choice but Nigel insisted. This situation was quite the challenge even for the seasoned pro. Even though Nasta had studied the files on her mark, she was quite nervous just the same.

This time she had met her match. His name was Claude St. Pierre, listed in M-16's files as one of the most elusive and dangerous criminals in the world. A master of disguise who never looked the same twice, Interpol had St. Pierre listed as a five foot nine with jet-black hair and a light complexion while the CIA described him as heavy set with light brown hair and piercing blue eyes. His weapon of choice was the collapsible crossbow as used in medieval times. This weapon had a tracking device concealed inside a compartment on the arrow. Ingenious and quite deadly, it was the ultimate sniper's weapon, capable of hitting its mark from three miles away. A perp could literally drink a cup of coffee then leave the scene with time to spare before anyone knew what happened. Last but not least, St. Pierre loved to use cunning and guile to lure his victim to the trap, perhaps by dressing up like a lady of the evening. Somehow he has killed someone while dressed like a prostitute. By kissing the victim on the mouth, when close enough, he would open a locket that released a deadly blade piercing the person's throat that would sever his jugular and kill him instantly. Nasta became ill every time she thought of such a heinous crime.

In their meeting to discuss the kill, Etlaw had showed little emotion about the job, like an old pro. Wary just the same, this young killer could be a detriment just as easily. Before they left for the theater, Etlaw had checked a shoulder bag that she was carrying. Inside was a black rose. *Interpol's number 3 assassin. This is the real deal. I could retire and disappear with this hit. Thirty million pounds of bounty on her head.* Some would wonder how they arrived at the figure. It's a combination of the now, who she is killing at the present, and the future based on the ease at which she is killing famous and well-guarded villains.

St. Pierre ambled along London's famous streets as if he were any common citizen. *Ambled* was the accurate description, for he was disguised as a three-hundred-pound well-dressed citizen. The only way for him to move along was to waddle or amble, moving along side to side like some out-of-place penguin. But don't be fooled for one second. St. Pierre trained for his profession somewhere in the Galapagos Islands, in a house where virtually the finest trackers in the world couldn't even get close to finding. Who would ever suspect anyone to live in this part of the world, for on these islands dwell creatures and their descendants from prehistoric times. St. Pierre was not your ordinary man.

Anastasia and Etlaw were privy to a secret file on this man that has every bit of info. There was approximately one page. They both looked at each other, holding their eye contact as one would do out of recognition. *No, no way, impossible*, he thought, *impossible*.

On the other hand, Nasta thought maybe he was coming on to her. "Not another," she cried. "I hope not." The night was growing longer, and they both were getting sleepy.

"Let's pick this up tomorrow," said Etlaw. "I will be fresher then, and we can go on to get this job finished."

Etlaw had a very restless sleep, tossing and turning, calling out the name of a woman, sweat drenching his nightshirt. "Marinnnnn—no, please let her live." He suddenly woke up, startled and confused. He got out of bed and wondered aloud, "Who the fuck is that girl? Where do I know her from?" He quickly dismissed the recognized feelings, contributing it to lack of sleep and way too much stress. Stress—the killer of men throughout the world.

"Please, Robert." Nigel pleaded with Robert to be extremely careful on this assignment and to cover Nasta's back. "Those two are off the charts, young lady. That means simply off the danger charts. They can't even be classified. They have seen and done it all. God knows that neither does their deed strictly for the money, both are rumored to own palatial properties all over the world, automobiles, and jewelry worth a king's fortune. Maybe, just maybe, that on this assignment each will eliminate one another. How crazy and absurd an idea," Nigel thought. "Perish the idea," said Nigel, continuing to talk to himself.

St. Pierre arrived at the Hotel Pergola at approximately two in the afternoon. As usual, deadly punctual. The hit was to take place at 5:00 p.m. in broad daylight. Highly trained assassins didn't care one way or another whether light or dark because they were experts at blending into the crowd, in this case, during rush-hour traffic in downtown London. St. Pierre, one of the richest, most powerful men in the world, drove up to the hotel in a black 1972 Volkswagen Beetle, a very, very recognizable car, but St. Pierre was never the worrier kind. He liked to play the game, to live dangerously, on the edge, always taking chances. On the other hand, Etlaw just wanted to get the hit over with, collect his pay, and hightail out of there and go home to his main residence, a Spanish villa on the Mediterranean Sea, just outside of Marbella.

*For some reason, something feels different today*, he thought to himself. *I just cannot put my finger on it. Ah, screw it. I will be a very rich man after this—very, very rich.* His mind was racing now, anticipating the hunt and finally the kill.

"Wow, I feel like a young buck, that dry feeling in the back of my throat, a little shaky in the knees, just a little more than usual that's all," he said to himself. "Merely a walk in the park."

Wembley Stadium was about ten minutes from his hotel.

This information was supplied by Nigel and his staff, so precise. Nasta, always a few minutes late, knew the tube schedule by heart, every single stop, the most efficient, punctual train in the civilized world, but still always late. Someday it could cost her her own life.

April weather in London was predictably damp and rainy, winter coats and jackets were common, perfect to conceal a weapon or several for that matter. Carefully concealed under her suede Gucci jacket was the weapon of her choice. For this prey, Nasta, with Nigel's approval, decided to kill him up close. Her weapon was a tiny, tiny blow dart, which was constructed in Africa by the ancient Urandu tribe. It could be hidden in one's mouth without detection. A sudden cough, the slightest opening of one's mouth, was enough to direct the poison projectile with precise accuracy right to the target. In just five short minutes, the victim would be dead, and Nasta could leave her black rose in the victim's jacket and get away. Etlaw's job and contribution was to conceal a hypodermic needle in his arm sleeve. As the victim fell to the sidewalk, Etlaw would assist in lowering the poison-laden body to the ground. Of course, as usual, he would be dressed in disguise. A disguise that even Nasta nor Nigel knew nothing about. Etlaw insisted on this arrangement just in case he decided to kill the Black Rose as well. *How perfect this is for me, she'll never know what hit her.* He already had three-fourths of the money, another insistence of his or else he wouldn't have accepted this foe. Nasta knew nothing of these matters.

Nasta was hurrying through the streets of London like a sprinter, first thirty meters in a lowered crouch as if she were running in a seated position. She could readily recall her trainer screaming, "Lower your waist, run sitting down. It's less noticeable when trying to escape the crime scene." Even though Nasta hated that man, she believed in his methodology. When she distanced herself far enough away from the kill zone, she then slipped into an alley, not randomly but one that was previously scouted and planned. In the blink of an eye, she pulled a tag on her sweater, and her outer layer of clothing pulled away entirely to reveal underclothing that of a marathon runner on a cold dreary London day. *Ingenious of Nigel*, she thought, *ingenious.*

So now Nasta was in the clear. Just your ordinary twentyish woman out for a run. Looking behind her once or twice to detect any followers, little did she know or even imagine that about two hundred yards ahead was Robert Etlaw. He had hailed a taxi, waiting for the right moment, the moment to assassinate the Black Rose, everyone's number 1 hire to kill in the entire world, and Etlaw had this marvelous opportunity to kill her and be hailed as the greatest for the short time he had remaining in his life.

According to plan, she was to keep running at a steady clip until she reached the bank of London on Juniper Street. There she was would duck into the crowd at the outdoor market and blend in unceremoniously, where no one suspected a thing. She quickly purchased a North Face jacket and became an average citizen. The steady sound of the police pierced the air; the bobbies were on their way, only to find a body with no clues.

Beads of perspiration streaming down his temples, mind racing, just like when he first started, he could recollect the days of his youth, and how he would get so nervous before a hit. At seventy-two years young, there were those same feelings. *It must be her, killing a woman, a young beautiful one at that.* Etlaw knew everything about the St. Pierre hit, something Nigel normally didn't allow, but this time, for some strange reason, he did. Now as the time drew near,

Etlaw would position himself in ready to pop out of an alley in Piccadilly and surprise the young killer. *A rose to a kill*, he thought. *How exciting*, he thought. Waiting, this waiting was driving him crazy, his mind racing even faster. *Come to me, Black Rose*, and in disguise, except for her face, Etlaw would drive a hunter's knife right through her heart and, with a curare edge, fauvist the knife until her death.

He peered at his Tag Heuer watch, clever edition. Just five more minutes and there, there at the corner no less than twenty meters away, there was the Black Rose. Etlaw now slipped back in the alley and concealed himself. Nasta, oblivious as to what was about to happen, suddenly stopped to tie her New Balance running shoes just about five yards short of Etlaw's kill zone. He quickly calculated the distance change leaped out of the shadows to execute his swansong and kill this wench. Everything seemed to be happening in slow motion. Etlaw drew his sword, about to pierce her heart, when as if by remote control, Etlaw's arms fell to his side, his mouth was wide open, spittle starting to form in his mouth corners, his last breath came with the word "youuuuu!" Just then, Nigel himself leaped out behind a parked Citron auto.

"He was going to kill you, Nasta. Thank God that the smell of greed hit my nostrils first, dear girl."

The body of Robert Etlaw was quickly removed from the scene a half an hour later. Plenty of time for Nigel and Nasta to get back to the compound.

Both were totally exhausted. Natural for her, Nasta started dropping the F bomb on every other word without exception. Nigel just stared into space, a rather confused look on his face. *Ummm*, thought Nasta. *I've seen him looking like that. I almost feel sorry for the bloke, but not too sorry.*

"Anastasia, I have something I must tell you. It cannot wait any longer, not one second."

"Okay, but I am so glad that mfefer is gone. He gave me the creeps. Sometimes he seemed to look right through me. Fuck him, he's dead and we aren't. Isn't that what you would want me to say? Finally, for the first time, that is exactly how I feel. He deserved to *die*."

"Sit down, my dear, and pour us both a glass of Port. You are old enough now, especially after today. About three years ago, Mr. Etlaw rung me on the telly, a first for him, sounding very drunk and very belligerent. He said, 'I saw an artist sketch of the great Black Rose. I noticed it on one of the inspector's desks over at Scotland Yard. You see, from time to time, I would go there and offer to clean the place from top to bottom for a mere six pence and a bottle of the finest twelve-year-old Scottie. They never asked for my credentials, strange, very strange. But anyway, I saw the scotch, and as soon as I laid eyes on her face, I knew I had seen her before, in a different circumstance of course.' Yes, indeed," Nigel thought aloud, "it was very peculiar conversation. The next day I went over to see my old friend Dr. Smite who does me quite a few favors. This time, my request seemed to startle him. 'That's a gray area, Nigel. I'll have to think about it further."

"What is the gray—"

"Quiet, just listen for once, can you do that for me?"

"Whoaaaa!" said Nasta. "Please go on, Sir Nigel."

"I finally convinced the doc to perform the task almost without reluctance. He liked the blood and guts, need I say more, and so did Etlaw. One evening, around midnight, one of the girls tipped me off that Etlaw and Dr. Smite had a nocturnal rendezvous the same night. Doc, syringe in hand, slipped into Etlaw's room and extracted a vial of blood and delivered it to me. 'Thank you, thank you, dear man. Will it be the usual Thursday?' 'Of course. Without the blood, old man, I say, cheerio.' It's a good thing old Etlaw is a heavy, heavy drinker and sleeper," smiled Nigel.

About a week passed before Nigel decided to have a look at the blood samples. *My curiosity is killing me! A-positive, unusual type*, thought Nigel. This guy was capable of anything to conceal his identity, but the blood tells all. Etlaw's blood in hand, Nigel decided to have a spot of tea. Nasta had risen early, already drinking her tea. As Nigel came around the corner, the swinging door hit Nasta in her hand, the one holding her tea. Porcelain splattered all over the kitchen floor. Nasta was barefoot. As she avoided one piece of the sharp broken teacup, she stepped on another. Blood was everywhere, and Nigel thought, *Why not have a look at her blood as well?* So he removed another vial from the lab and took Nasta's blood sample. *I feel like a vampire*, he thought to himself. Of course, Nasta knew nothing of his intentions; she was too busy removing glass from her feet. Because of her callous, she wasn't hurt that bad. Just some blood.

Nasta went out shopping, and the wife and kids were off to the country to see his in-laws. *The perfect time*, he thought, *just perfect*. He slowly removed both vials and placed them in two separate flasks. The first was from Etlaw, still A-positive, no surprise. The second flask—just that moment, Nasta entered the house through the backdoor. She could hear the echo of his voice, screaming.

Nigel never saw it coming; the bullet struck his left temple, shattering his skull, killing him instantly.

Nasta managed to escape to parts unknown with reason to kill again.

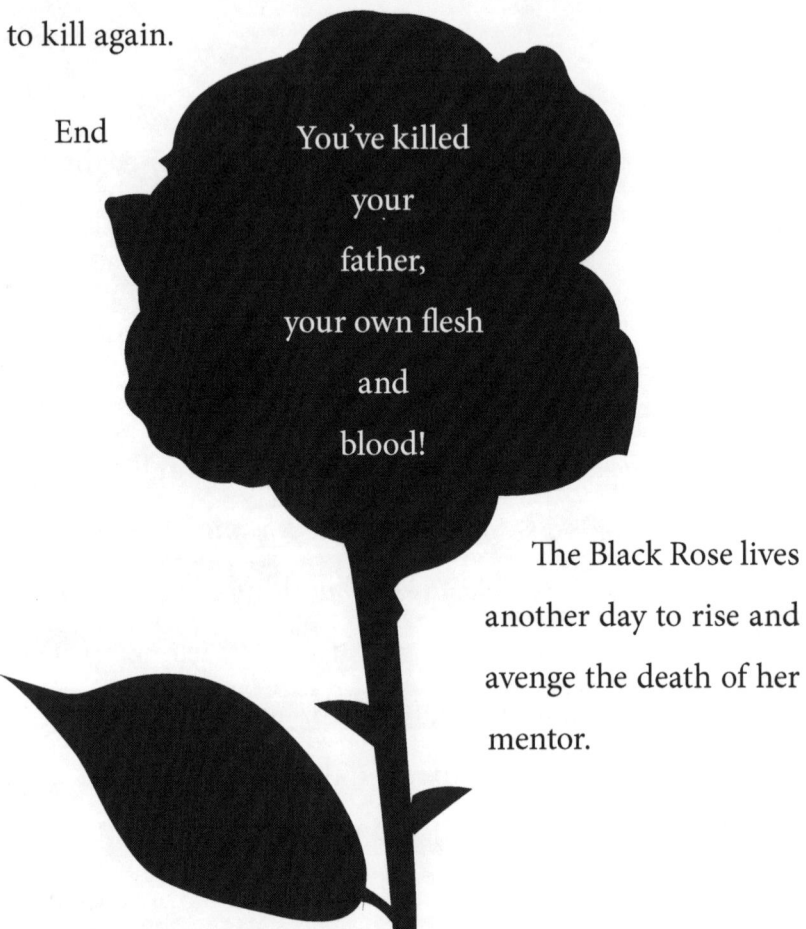

End

You've killed your father, your own flesh and blood!

The Black Rose lives another day to rise and avenge the death of her mentor.

Made in the USA
Lexington, KY
29 May 2013